1632 & Beyond Issue #8

1632 & Beyond, Garrett W. Vance, Terry Howard, Edith Wild, Bethanne Kim, Bjorn Hasseler, Aaron Jameison Greso

Flint's Shards, Inc.

ERIC FLINT'S 1632 & BEYOND ISSUE #8

This is a work of fiction. Names, characters places, and events portrayed in this book are fictional or used fictitiously. Any resemblance to real people (living or dead), events, or places is coincidental.

Editor-in-Chief Bjorn Hasseler
Head of Operations Bethanne Kim
Editor Chuck Thompson
Interior Artwork by Garrett W. Vance

1. Science Fiction-Alternate History
2. Science Fiction-Time Travel

eBook ISBN: 978-1-962398-14-5
Paperback ISBN: 978-1-962398-15-2

Distributed by Flint's Shards Inc.
339 Heyward Street, #200
Columbia, SC 29201

Other 1632 Universe Publications

1632 by Eric Flint created this universe. Free download available at Baen
.com/1632.html. All listed books available at Baen.com.

Short-List of Titles to Jump into the Series:

Ring of Fire anthology edited by Eric Flint

1633 by Eric Flint and David Weber

1634: The Baltic War by Eric Flint and David Weber

All books available through Baen.com, booksellers, and used book-
stores.

Also Available:

Grantville Gazette Volumes 1 – 102, magazine edited by Eric Flint, Paula
Goodlett, Walt Boyes, Bjorn Hasseler. Available on 1632Magazine.com.

1632 Universe novels and "Eric Flint, Ring of Fire Series" on Baen.com

Recently Released:

1635: The Weavers Code by Eric Flint and Jody Lynn Nye

Ongoing: Baen is re-releasing select 1632 books originally released by
Eric Flint's Ring of Fire Press, starting with Bjorn Hasseler's NESS books.
Please check the Baen.com e-arc bundles and new releases regularly!

Odd numbered months: New issues of Eric Flint's 1632 & Beyond

Forthcoming:

1637: The French Correction by Eric Flint and Walter Hunt

1637: The Pacific Initiative by Iver P. Cooper

Contents

Eric Flint's 1632 & Beyond Issue #8

The Magdeburg Messenger

(1632 Fiction)

This issue's theme is ongoing adventures. Once we come to the end of a story, our characters don't just stop; they go on about their lives. Four of our stories center around characters you already know, and the authors of the other two already plan to revisit their characters.

The cover art is from "How Lovely Are Thy Branches" by Garrett W. Vance. It's romance and finding a Christmas tree in the Wonderland Isles.

"Rites of Passage" is Edith Wild's fourth story about Amalia von Herbert and Maggie Vogel. Their previous story, in *1632 & Beyond* Issue 4, ended on a cliffhanger. ~~We're sorry about that.~~ Come see what happens next!

"A Week Together" by Bjorn Hasseler finds Reed and Kathy Sue Burroughs is home while Reed is between wars.

Aaron Jamieson Greso's first 1632 story is "The Diablo Is In The Details." A merchant and a knight, both Portuguese, are trying buy compasses and sell a donkey, two tasks that are harder than anticipated.

The new timeline is so different that sometimes a problem is exactly the opposite of what we expect. "Emancipation and Education" is Terry Howard's story about a boy who wants to stay *in* school against his father's wishes.

Skip has given the girl a stiletto. Now it's catching on, and in Bethanne Kim's "Stilettos, Part 2," he's got a plan to make more.

Editors' Notes

With this issue, we're extending *Eric Flint's 1632 & Beyond* to 50,000 words, at the same cost.

We've got something else for you, too. After Ring of Fire Press closed, Baen Books acquired a couple dozen of the 1632 books published there. Those have been coming out monthly. The Available Now and Coming Soon columns will keep you up to date.

One of the books that was not acquired is *A 1632 Christmas*. We have approached those authors, and all have agreed: *Eric Flint's 1632 & Beyond* will publish two special issues. Each will have ten of the stories from *A 1632 Christmas*. Our goal is to publish the first in November and the second in December. The twenty-first story is a Marla and Franz story by David Carrico, and that's going to be included with the other Marla & Franz stories in the reissue of *1635: Music and Murder*, also coming in December.

Characters from the first three stories in this issue also appear in stories in the Christmas issues.

Magdeburg Messenger
Fiction

Flint's Shards, Inc.

How Lovely Are Thy Branches
Garrett W. Vance

Dodo Island, The Wonderland Isles Colonies
December 21, 1637

It was just before sunrise as Pers finished up his simple breakfast of bread, cheese, and a thin slice of dried beef. Having grown up at sea, he had never developed a taste for what he thought of as fancy foods. Pers preferred a diet of simple dishes similar to the fare served to sailing men, but thankfully without any weevils.

Dorothea Weise, Director of the Wonderland Isles Colonial Natural Resource and Wildlife Service, entered Pam's Bird Barn like a sliver of the rising morning sun, her ever-radiant beauty and positive energy lighting up the cavernous gloom.

"Did I interrupt your breakfast?"

"No, not at all!" As ever, Pers was very glad to see her, always eager to bask in her glow. Sometimes at night he wondered if her presence in his life was just a pleasant dream, only to be reassured by her morning arrivals. "Would you like some coffee?"

"Oh yes, thank you!" She sat down at the table with an eager expression on her face. "Pers, you make the best coffee!" she exclaimed as he filled her mug. The steaming hot, aromatic brew was made from native coffee trees the founder of the colony and their revered mentor, Pam Miller, had discovered in the mountains behind Castaway Cove.

"I can't take credit for it. Pam taught me everything I know on the subject." His reply caused Dorothea to laugh and roll her eyes at his modesty. This was a debate they often shared—Dorothea always insisted that Pers' talents were not all dependent on his adopted mother's teachings, while Pers quietly remained as humble as could be. Before it could get started, Pers deftly steered the conversation away from himself and back to the drink at hand.

"According to Pam, the morning 'cup of Joe' is a tradition held quite dear in Grantville. They can't start the day without it. Now I find I feel that way myself!"

"Me, too!" Dorothea exclaimed. She blew on the hot liquid to cool it, and to Pers' surprise, began to drink it as rapidly as she could, to the point that he was afraid she might burn her tongue instead of savoring the cup as she usually did.

Observing this unusual behavior he couldn't help but ask, "Dorothea, what's on your mind today?"

Dorothea paused in her attack on the hot coffee to blow in and out quickly in an attempt to cool down her mouth, to the extent that she rather comically resembled a gasping fish. Pers hid any sign of mirth as he patiently waited for her answer. Once she had sufficiently lowered the temperature behind her appealingly rosy lips, she exclaimed, "Christmas! We have to get ready for our party, and I need your help."

Pers, who would do anything she asked, even if it was something hazardous to his own health and well-being (which she mercifully never did ask, of course), straightened up in his chair and proclaimed, "Sure! Just tell me what you need!"

"We need to find a Christmas tree!"

Pers gave a small frown.

"Dorothea, last Christmas Pam complained that there weren't any species here on the island fit for the tradition. They're usually conifers like pines and firs, aren't they?"

Dorothea's demeanor dampened somewhat as she considered that statement. "Yes, I suppose I hadn't thought of that." She frowned. Generally, Dorothea thought of *everything*; the bright young woman was an undisputed genius.

Pers instantly regretted the rain he had sprinkled on her parade. His long, lanky form shifted uncomfortably in his chair, a physical manifestation of the anxiety that filled his mind. *What to do?* he asked himself. Dorothea's distress, as mild as it might be, was extremely worrying to the devoted Pers, her greatest admirer. *Think of something!*

Suddenly, an idea came to him.

"Must it be a conifer? There are a great many trees on the island. Perhaps we could find something else that would work?" Another thought came into his head just then, which he immediately squelched—*and the vast majority of those are heavily protected, and we are their protectors! Cutting down a tree was not a casual affair on Dodo Island.* The very thought made him stiffen slightly. *Well, at least we can just write our own permit....*

Dorothea carefully considered Pers' words with her finely arched brows furrowed in thought, an expression Pers always found utterly charming. After a moment of deliberation, and to Pers' great relief, the smile returned to her face.

"I don't suppose it must be a conifer. It just has to be about eight feet tall, pretty, and smell nice." They had recently encountered a grove of *Foetidia Mauritianao,* or *stinkwood,* in their travels about the island, an attractive-enough-looking tree that more than lived up to its name. "I can think of a few native trees that might fit the bill. We will just have to go and have a look." Dorothea finished her cup of coffee in one prodigious gulp (it had, thankfully, cooled down enough to make that safe to do), jumped up from her chair, and headed for the door. "Whenever you are ready, Mr. Secretary!" she added with a sunny smile as she exited the building.

Pers waited until she was out of sight before he grimaced at her use of his official title, for which he still felt he was egregiously unqualified. Back when his adopted mother Pam Miller was governor of the colony, she had appointed Pers to be the Wonderland Secretary of the Interior, despite the fact that he had spent most of his young life out at sea. He knew she had done so because she trusted him implicitly to carry on her conservationist policies and to continue to protect the island's iconic dodo birds that had become extinct in her former future world. But he also suspected her penchant for irony had played a part in it as well.

Knowing that the highly energetic Dorothea would be up and at it early as she always was, Pers was already dressed and ready to go. The morning's original plan had been to do a timber survey in the great forests that surrounded the town, so looking for a Christmas tree would be an easy addition. Raised as a ship's cabin boy, Pers didn't have much experience with the holiday that excited Dorothea so greatly. He just hoped he would be able to grant her wish and find a suitable Christmas tree for her. It was now his most solemn duty to do so. If only he had a better idea as to what local species might prove acceptable. Off the top of his head, he couldn't think of seeing anything that remotely resembled a fir or a pine on the island....

"Hey, are you coming?" Dorothea popped her head back through the door, the morning sun edging her lush brown curls with gold. The angelic sight of her and the sweet sound of her bell-like voice snapped Pers out of his reverie. He leaped out of his chair and stood at attention just as he would at the call of his Swedish Navy commanders.

"Yes, of course! I will get the ax."

Dorothea paused to give him a pixieish smile. "No, not an *ax*, Pers! Bring a *shovel!* We are going to keep our Christmas tree alive, then plant it on the grounds here at the institute after the holiday. It will be so much fun!"

Pers smiled back, but couldn't help but think ruefully to himself, *it looks like you have some hard labor ahead of you today, deckhand! Ah well, it is all for a good cause.* Pers would gladly dig up a mighty oak with a soup spoon if Dorothea asked it of him. Knowing well the ever-professional policies of the dedicated Dorothea, they would get their scheduled survey done with the search for a Christmas tree tacked onto it. Pers allowed himself a small chuckle as he stopped by the tool rack near the door. *"Fun," she says.* Notably he was the one carrying the shovel.

Dorothea stood in the Bird Barn's well-kept garden with her arms stretched out at her sides as she absorbed the rich, dawn light that bathed the island, a wide smile on her face. It was plain that she was extremely excited about her project. She exclaimed, "Pers, this is your chance to enjoy another Christmas tradition! Finding the proper tree is always a treat we Germans look forward to."

Pers nodded dutifully. He knew full well who would be given the treat of digging up a living tree by the roots.

Pers stepped out into the balmy December morning in the height of the Antipodean summer and was greeted by a welcome sight—an old friend waited to join their expedition, a sturdy Swedish farm horse named Olle. The large, dark brown, black-maned fellow patiently browsed the verdant grass that grew around the picnic table. The Department of the Interior often borrowed Olle from their neighbor, Jens Hansson, a friendly farmer who lived just down the broad meadow from the Institute. Olle helped them out with heavy tasks, which he performed dutifully and without complaint. Dorothea rubbed his shaggy mane affectionately while giving him an apple, which he demolished in the blink of an eye.

Pers, as possibly the hardest-working Secretary of the Interior in the world, would have some extra muscle at his disposal today and was most grateful for it. Olle would be there to help him pull an as-yet-unidentified tree out of the earth and drag it back to town. There it was Dorothea's plan to pot it in a suitably sized barrel, then decorate it for the celebration. Shortly after New Year's, the tree would be replanted in a suitable location in the Bird Barn's gardens, where it would provide a pleasant, living reminder of what was shaping up to be a season to be remembered.

Pers strapped the shovel onto Olle's wide back, then, in thanks for him taking on that particular burden, gave him a handful of nuts. He always kept some in his pockets for Dodo Island's ever-hungry namesakes, who had now evolved into savvy beggars. *"Get ready for a long day, old chum!"* he whispered into the horse's furry ear.

An hour later they hiked through the cool, verdant expanse of the ancient forest, untouched by human hands, and in this new timeline, destined to mostly remain so. There would have to be some logging, yes, but only in a very sustainable and non-destructive way. This was their goal today, identifying areas with trees that could stand some thinning without harming the overall ecosystem. Pam's personal theory was that, in her native up-time, deforestation caused the dodo's demise more than the birds being eaten by hungry sailors. The island had been practically clear-cut for its valuable timber, destroying the nuts that were a major part of the dodos' diet. Simply put, the poor things had starved to death—something that definitely would not happen now.

As they went, Pers did his best to help locate the proper Christmas tree candidate among the many denizens of the well-foliated environs. Dorothea would take a moment to study his suggestions, but then regretfully shake her head and tell him, "No, I'm sorry, Pers. It's close, but still not quite the right one," and move on to the next grove. Pers had to admit to himself that his picks were based more on signs that a tree might be relatively easy to free from the ground than its actual visible charms and eventually gave up, content just to follow quietly along with his good pal Olle.

They eventually stopped for lunch at the edge of a small clearing, the living green canopy providing a pleasant natural parasol. It was hot today, full summer in the Southern Hemisphere, which was taking the transplanted northern folk a bit of getting used to. Pam, with the help of the well-liked and respected Doctor Durand, had issued stern warnings to the colonists about overexposure to the Tropic of Capricorn's midday sun, something the Swedes simply weren't used to dealing with. Despite such admonitions, their first year on Dodo Island had seen enough cases of heat exhaustion and sunburns to keep the good doctor very busy treating the poor fools who hadn't heeded his warnings. The number of those afflicted had come down as the stubbornly hard-working colonists finally accepted the notion that they needed to take a midday break from outdoor labors and find something to do in the shade until the intense heat of the day had passed.

As always, Dorothea had taken it upon herself to prepare them both an excellent trail lunch, a kindness that Pers very much appreciated, and yet another example of the young woman's many admirable talents and traits. Pers took care of Olle with a wooden bowl of water from a skin attached to his back, a double handful of oats, and an apple to supplement the natural vegetation he occasionally paused to sample throughout the day. Meanwhile, Dorothea had spread out their luncheon on a cheerful blue-and-white checkered picnic cloth.

Having Olle along to carry their lunch had ensured that the offerings were more expansive than usual, and Pers, although he avowed to a spartan diet, couldn't help but feel a ravenous hunger at the very sight of the edible delights laid before him. There was a salad of cucumber and spring onions in a peppercorn-spiced vinegar dressing, small sandwiches made of thinly sliced brown bread with smoked fish, onion, and fresh mayonnaise, deviled eggs made with mustard and minced radish, fried chicken seasoned with rosemary and thyme, and a pile of sumptuous sweet pudding pretzels for dessert.

His "Momma Pam" had often made sure to point out to Pers that Dorothea was a damn fine cook, always with a certain freighted meaning that was more than just a compliment to the young woman's extensive culinary abilities. Shy Pers always pretended not to catch her nuances, but inwardly it was all part of his utter fascination and devotion to the amazing heavenly creature named Dorothea Weise.

"I made your favorites today, Pers. I hope you like them," she told him. She settled onto the grass beside him with her knees bent and legs folded under her ever-captivating frame.

"Wow, Dorothea!" he exclaimed in Grantville-style English, "You sure put on a spread! What a feast!"

Dorothea smiled brightly at his compliment and performed an entrancing shrug of the shoulders and toss of her head that made Pers pause to catch his breath. She always had this kind of effect on him. Her every move was intoxicating, and even though she made him dizzy, all he ever wanted was more.

"Do you really think so?" She looked up to catch him in the gaze of her luminous hazel eyes.

Pers, quite unable to control himself, had already tucked in and rather embarrassingly had to assure her around a mouthful of delightful deviled egg. "Oh yesh, I do! Shank you!"

She laughed at his garbled answer and proceeded to dig in herself. They had both developed a healthy appetite during the morning's strenuous hike. Pers paused to quietly watch her eat for a moment. Even the simplest of daily tasks utterly captivated him. *She made my favorites.* He took a moment to consider what that might mean. *That's a good thing, right? If she likes me enough to take all the trouble to do that, maybe....*

He stopped himself there. It was best not to think too hard on such matters, but focus on maintaining his calm in the maelstrom of feelings that swirled within him. He was afraid to let her see how much he really thought of her, afraid that it would somehow break the magic spell that kept them together as, without a doubt, something more than just amicable colleagues. She was his friend, and a true one, but anything beyond that was just too much to hope for. With an effort, he pushed his dreams aside and went back to devouring the feast she had prepared, incredibly pleased and amazed that she had done so just for him.

Once the meal had ended, Pers showered her with compliments on its excellent quality and swore he couldn't eat another bite, even though a lone pudding pretzel remained uneaten. Dorothea promised to wrap it for his breakfast, but somehow it ended up in Olle's eager belly, which Pers didn't feel at all slighted by—she would make more! They resumed their search for the perfect (or at least acceptable) Christmas tree. Dorothea allowed as to how the tropical ecology was not lending itself to this task and lamented the lack of proper boreal conifers, but refused to give up.

Pers was somewhat relieved when Dorothea declared they would change course and begin to head back toward town on a different path than the one they had followed to this point. Pers was well used to physically demanding tasks under harsh conditions from his years at sea. This wasn't so bad, and he contented himself with following along behind Dorothea, (who somehow never seemed to tire herself) enjoying the pleasant views of her lithe form's shapely posterior. Occasionally, provocative thoughts rose to the surface of the tranquil sea of his mind like hot bubbles from a deep thermal vent of desire, but he poked them back as quickly as they came, striving to remain pure in his chivalrous devotion to the enchanting sylph that flitted through the forest before him.

After another long hour of fruitless searching, Dorothea came to a stop a few yards ahead of him and stood staring raptly at a certain tree, an expression of delight on her ever-lovely face. Pers looked at the tree from a somewhat different perspective— it was quite a bit more than eight feet tall, pushing nine or ten. The Christmas-tree-to-be was an abundantly foliaged *Diospyros egrettarum,* white-barked branches clad in large, glossy leaves. With a silent groan Pers saw that its roots were well ensconced in hard, rocky soil. It was going to require some heavy work to dig it out of there, and he was the guy who was going to have to do it.

"Oh look, Pers, isn't it beautiful? The leaves in that deep shade of green remind me of holly, and what delightful white bark! It practically cries out 'Christmas' as it is, without even being decorated yet!" She looked over at Pers, who quickly changed his facial expression from resigned dread to encouraging agreement.

"It is lovely. If you are sure this is the one, shall I begin?"

"Oh, yes, I am sure, so please do." She paused as a worried expression replaced the simple joy her face had held previously. "You know, it is awfully big. Are you sure you can dig it out, Pers? Is it too much to handle? Maybe I could take a turn?"

Pers grinned and was quick to laugh that off. "Of course not! Nothing an able seaman like myself can't manage! Just relax, and I will see to it." He spoke the truth. Over the last year Pers had grown from an awkward teen into the veritable definition of a strapping young man, although at times he still felt very much awkward.

Dorothea looked relieved at his effusive expression of confidence. "Okay, I know you are a strong man, Pers, so I won't worry. But it's awfully hot out, so do be careful!"

"Hot? Not as hot as a foredeck under the full sun at the equator! We're mostly in the shade here! Paradise!"

They both laughed at his cheerful nonchalance. She turned back to the tree and raised her arms as if to embrace it. To Pers' surprise and delight she began to sing in her melodious alto voice— *"O Tannenbaum, O Tannenbaum, Du kannst mir sehr gefallen!"*

Pers smiled at the old carol. He had heard Pam sing it in English the year before. He suddenly found himself singing, *"O Christmas tree, O Christmas tree, How lovely are thy branches,"* while he helplessly stared at her, drinking in her captivating countenance.

Dorothea looked over at him with a delighted expression on her face as she realized Pers' gaze was placed directly on her, not the tree. She laughed and asked him in a coy tone, "Do you really think so, Pers? Are my branches lovely?" while she stretched her lithe arms above her head as if she were a magical dryad returning to her arboreal form.

This bit of teasing had the effect of making Pers' face flush an alarmed scarlet. He coughed and managed to respond with a croaked, "Sure I do!" before he shyly fled the scene to retrieve the shovel from Olle's broad back. He lingered there a few moments, taking some deep breaths to calm himself and to avoid any further ribbing from Dorothea. He heard her laugh merrily before she returned to her quiet admiration of their Christmas-tree-to-be.

Pers shook off the last of his embarrassment, then girded himself for the exertion to come. He walked once around the tree to find the best spot to begin the excavation. There really wasn't one, so he shrugged and thrust his shovel in at the point nearest to him. The ground was indeed hard and rocky, and he only penetrated a few inches.

"Are you really sure about this, Pers? It looks awfully hard." Dorothea's tone had once again turned to concern.

"Oh, it's nothing. I'll be done in a blink of the eye!" He even hazarded a comical wink at her, which made her laugh again, a music more lovely than any ancient yuletide carol to Pers' adoring ears.

Two hours of hard labor later, Pers was finally making some headway. It was so hot he had no choice but to take off his sweat-drenched shirt and hang it on a convenient shrub to dry. He apologized to the lady present for exposing himself, modestly though it may be. She responded with a funny kind of smile and told him, "Oh, I don't mind, Pers. I *really* don't" in what might possibly be construed as a coquettish tone. She then proceeded to watch him work in a way that somehow made him blush mightily. Fortunately, his face was already red from exertion so she wouldn't know. *Does she like what she sees?* He allowed himself to wonder, just for a moment, before he forced himself to concentrate on the task at hand.

A bit later, a small flock of dodos quietly emerged from the forest to stare at the proceedings with their disconcerting yellow eyes, which made Pers frown mightily as he toiled. Dorothea threw them some nuts to eat from her knapsack. Like practically everyone on the island, she always carried treats for the goofy things. They swiftly gobbled them up, then returned to watching Pers work, which somehow made his task even more taxing.

Pers had once referred to the dodos as "stupid creatures." After all, their name was thought to have been derived from the Portuguese word *doudo* which meant fool, but he had come to revise his opinion of their intelligence upwards after a few years of coexisting with them. They were perhaps the most beguiling beggars the world had ever seen, and the people of Port Looking Glass eagerly threw them handouts whenever they happened to be around or under foot, which was most of the time.

When he thought Dorothea was out of earshot, Pers hissed *"Shoo!"* at them, but they ignored him and continued to observe his efforts, thinking whatever it was that dodos thought about as they witnessed the busy doings of humanity—most likely their chances of another handout. Eventually coming to the conclusion that they weren't going to get any joy from the sweaty fellow in the pit, they wandered back into the forest as silently as they had come.

Pers bid them a fond farewell in his native Swedish by hissing, *"Bra ridning, ni dumma varelser!* Good riddance, you stupid creatures!" Out of the corner of his eye he saw Dorothea glance up at the sound, but her grasp of *Svenska* was still pretty basic. "Cute, aren't they?" Pers exclaimed in English with a bright smile, then returned to his digging with renewed vigor.

Another hour later, a very tired Pers paused to examine the state of the project. He had cleared most of the dirt from the roots and was finally ready to enlist the aid of Olle's horsepower. He wrapped a rope firmly around the base of the tree's trunk, then attached the other end to Olle's plow harness.

"Okay, Olle, your turn! Heave ho!" Olle knew exactly what to do and took a few careful steps forward with his large, thick hooves. The tree shifted, but then caught on something in the hole. Pers sighed, unsheathed the Bowie knife (a gift from Momma Pam) from his belt, and proceeded to lower himself into the hole as the roots scraped his bare chest. The tree was still connected to a tap root that ran deep into the rocky ground. Pers was pretty sure it would grow back in its new home, so he cut it as close to the bottom as he could, hoping he didn't kill the damn thing by doing so. He then lifted the tree from the bottom to give Olle a better angle to pull from.

"All right, Olle, heave!" he shouted, and the well-trained horse began to pull again. Inch by inch the tree slid upwards to the sound of Pers' grunts and Olle's heavy, expelled breaths as man and horse exerted themselves with all their strength to dislodge the stubborn thing from its dwelling.

The sounds woke up Dorothea, who had fallen asleep with her back against a massive ebony tree's broad trunk while she took notes on the day's activities. After a moment of disorientation, she remembered where she was and focused on the task unfolding before her eyes.

"Oh! Oh my! You almost have it!" She sprang to her feet.

"Heave, Olle, heave ho!" Pers shouted encouragement to his equine helper. With a few more grunts they finally succeeded in bringing the tree to the surface, where it lay on its side. It reminded Pers of a big salmon lying on the deck, helpless and destined to be dinner. Pers thought that if trees could talk it would be giving them a piece of its mind, and that piece would not be pleasant. Pers couldn't blame it for that; he would feel sorry for it, except that he was too tired to feel much of anything. He laid out a sturdy burlap tarp on the ground. With some help from Dorothea, who was to Pers' mind surprisingly strong for such a fair maiden, he rolled the tree onto the tarp, which would protect it as they dragged it home. After some more fussing about arranging the tow ropes, they were ready to go.

Pers was a mess, covered in dirt from head to toe. Dorothea made a fretful kind of clucking sound as she did her best to brush the worst of it off. The feel of her deft, smooth hands on his bare torso sent a jolt of electricity through him that made him tremble, but he was too exhausted to struggle, or, for that matter, to really enjoy the attention.

Dorothea returned his shirt to him, then made him drink some water. She gave Olle some water as well. The grateful horse lapped it up eagerly. After a short rest, they were recovered enough to begin the long trek home.

It was well after dark when they finally arrived at the Bird Barn on its hillside perch in the wide meadows above Port Looking Glass. The town's lights reflected perfectly on the mirror-smooth waters of the tranquil Indian Ocean bay it was built on. The cheerful sight made Dorothea smile. What a wonderful place to live and be young in, a Wonderland indeed!

Pers lay on the tarp with an arm around the tree trunk, fast asleep. He had claimed that he just needed a moment's rest, but once it became apparent he wouldn't be waking up any time soon, Dorothea simply had Olle continue on, dragging Pers along with the tree. Mighty Olle didn't seem to mind the extra weight as he eagerly devoured the apples Dorothea gave him in payment for his services.

Dorothea sent one of her flock of ever-eager-to-help University of Jena grad students to go get Olle's owner Herr Hanson and also ask for some able-bodied men from the village to help her finish the project. Pers was lifted by coarse, but gentle hands and taken directly to his bed, dirty as he was. Dorothea would see to having his laundry done and his bedclothes changed out in the morning. She pulled a light blanket over him, then sat beside him for a few minutes, wiping his sleeping face with a cool, damp cloth.

"Good work, brave Pers. You truly are my Christmas angel!" she told him, but he was too deep in dreams to hear— dreams of her, and sweet ones.

Rites of Passage
Edith Wild

By Edith Wild

*A*malia von Herbert and Maggie Vogel have appeared in three previous stories:

"A Christmas Stollen" in A 1632 Christmas

"Leftovers" in Grantville Gazette 100

"A Knight's Tale – Therapies" in 1632 & Beyond Issue 4

Herr Johannes Esslie's Math Classroom, Grantville High School
After School, February 2, 1637

Johannes Esslie did not want to leave home this afternoon, but he had to set up student work, those math tests for tomorrow. He was always thankful that the high school's administration did not mind this arrangement. Good will only lasted so long. He did not want to disturb it.

Affording Grantville, with all his medical costs, was impossible just now.

The ancient boarding house's age surpassed that of the fortified lodge a few miles farther away. The lodge was as much of a *mehr als nur ein Jagdschloss,* six centuries old, to the boarding house's claim of eight centuries of occupancy. It was *"The Saale River House,"* as the faded sign freshly but badly painted in two languages said. The Saale River was simply east, below the boarding house. Down a ramp to the river's edge was a small series of empty docks sticking out into the Saale.

The boarding house was a *wirtschaft* on the ground floor, a good anonymous place, if a man cared to be so. The kitchen and court to the north were even older, and the stable behind those was the last piece of an even older building, maybe even early medieval. Everything where the stone wasn't visible was plastered in an off-white smear.

The yellow "bus" stopped as usual in front of the ancient boarding house. The team of horses whined and snorted. Johannes boarded the horse-drawn bus along with the others as usual.

Johannes struggled with keeping his balance as the workhorses pulled the rattling yellow bus over the ice-lumped macadam run from Rudolstadt. The left side of his knee knocked into the edge of the bench seat he stood next to while he clung to the back of the seat on his right side. Some of the other packed-in passengers kept proving sharp elbows were annoying. The workhorse-drawn town buses were always standing room only. It was the convenient choice. Once onto Grantville's Route 250, the ride smoothed out enough. There were a few stops before the high school and after.

The road *into* Grantville was more passable when icy, but this was not the case once in Grantville. The roads in the Ring of Fire were *too* modern, *too* flat, *too* smooth. The yellow-painted wooden bus, even with good workhorses, slid and skidded as it went west on Route 250, somehow following the curve and not running off into the snowbanks lining the road. It was terrifying. Johannes was sure the horses hated it, as the load was always unbalanced.

The bus driver, a local woman whose name Johannes had never heard in all the time he'd been riding the bus, reined in the horses sharply. They slid to the next stop, in the bus loop of the high school. She shouted in English, then Amideutsch, "All out who's going out!"

Probably eight people, including him, piled out. As he went by the driver, Johannes said, "*Danke*."

She glared, relaxed, then said, "*Bitte*." Rolled her eyes. Then grinned.

Johannes climbed down the steps and off the bus. The horses stomped their feet, jittery. The icy patch after the bottom step had him skidding to his knees. His baseball cap fell off his head and onto the ice. He snatched the cap up, struggling to his feet.

Johannes labored over the incline, breathing hard, limping up it, both knees aching. He was thankful that he did feel somewhat better today. *It has to be the antibiotics,* he thought. Once at the top, he glanced back at Route 250. The bus was moving west into town, as normal.

He turned back to the tech center and the high school. From where he was, it was a modest distance to the high school door next to the tech center. He shivered. He was, no pun intended, cooling his heels and damned impatient over the wait in the cold. Too many people! None of the students rushing by noticed him. Or maybe they were ignoring him. *Am I that unrecognizable?*

Somehow, he breathed in wrong, caught a fragment of something. Then the misery of coughing started again.

Johannes didn't stop coughing for some time. The cough's *slight* whoop made him breathe harder, cough more. Somehow, in the background, there was a loud boom then a not-so-distant peppering and sputtering of something else. He barely heard *that* noise over his agonizing cough.

He spat a bit into a snowbank, sputum vaguely discolored. It was better than what it had been a few days back. He'd spent enough time coughing then spewing mucus, sometimes thick and stringy, sometimes almost black. It was not blood anymore! That *bloodiness* had been why he'd gone to actually see a doctor, finally, in November.

Those loud sounds were still there as he caught his breath. *Fireworks? Is there a party? It's Candlemas after all, so they're not Catholic.* It seemed a bit odd in the timing. It wasn't dark enough for fireworks. He did not see any bright flashes of fireworks either, so maybe they were small ones.

Johannes straightened up. The crowd of students was now just a trickle. He walked to the high school's doorway and slipped inside.

Johannes kept his scarf over his face as he walked through the halls. He wanted to avoid anyone he knew, as he'd done for over a dozen weeks—since early November. Too long. He padded inside the mailroom, looked around. No one was there, so while picking up his stack of copies he was not interrupted by explanations. He waved at his fellow teachers a distance away. They waved back.

He stopped by the cafeteria, poked into the kitchen. It was Candlemas, so Ludwiga had likely left early for that reason.

Johannes asked gently, throat raw, "Did Ludwiga set anything aside for me, Frau Böhm?"

The old woman grinned at him, pointing to a table at the end of the school's kitchen. "Look, see with eyes. There, bespoke for thee. 'Tis hot. I warn you."

"I see," he said. "*Ihr Englisch wird jedes mal besser, wenn wir sprechen.*"

"Ha! Take the tea also. Thou *ist* better, no?"

"I am not certain if I am better." He shrugged. "Thank you for the tea and food, Frau Böhm," Johannes said. He bowed slightly.

After a moment Frau Böhm said firmly, "Timotheus shall carry for thee." Her eyes were narrowed, observing him. She motioned to someone behind her.

"*Danke*, Frau."

The boy, Timotheus, thin, wide-eyed, young, maybe around fourteen, maybe not, silent, ended up taking the twine-tied stack of papers and the thermos of tea, then waiting. The boy was almost new to Johannes.

Johannes asked, "I've seen you around. Are you always quiet, Timotheus?"

"Speak to the man," said Frau Böhm.

The boy nodded, swallowed. He said softly to Johannes, "I follow you, Herr. I stay quiet?" He waited for a moment and asked, "Are soldiers shooting outside?"

"I do not think anyone is shooting. Fireworks maybe." Johannes carried his food. Timotheus trailed him to his classroom, left the papers and the thermos of tea on his desk, bowed slightly, and left. His boots made no sound. Johannes was never certain of anyone's background. The youth was afraid to speak, to say more, and had *that* look about him. He considered which social class the boy had been a part of before the siege of Magdeburg, before the slaughter. The boy had obviously not fared well, but he was alive. Which was better than most anyone who'd been there. *I should ask Frau Böhm about that boy, Timotheus. Hmm.*

Johannes knew that if the atrocity at Magdeburg hadn't killed you in any of a hundred ways, or the disease and starvation which followed, then the loss of status might do it. Over twenty thousand people at Magdeburg begged for mercy from Tilly and his commanders and soldiers, then they'd been murdered. *Those monsters,* he thought, *wiped my good city almost from the face of the Earth. The cannons demolished that piece of wall and it was done!*

I ran as the wall fell.

He shoved the memories of Magdeburg away into his darkness. *I came here for the mercy of it*, he thought. *I lived.* Johannes took his gloves off, dropped them on his desk, draped his cloak across the back of the chair. He crossed the room, cracked open one of the classroom's windows to let some fresh air in. He heard the popping, distantly.

Until the doctors were absolutely sure this thing eating away at him for these last months was not infectious, Johannes was staying away from others, or at least letting the air wash in.

He pulled his scarf and baseball cap off, dropped them on the corner of his desk. Eating in the cold was better than leaving bad air behind him. He had no appetite most days. The cook had been kind enough to save a small container of lunch leftovers and make a thermos of tea for him. That was a blessing. He ate a few bites of warm pot roast. The food stayed comfortably put, thank God. He sipped the hot herbal tea sweetened with honey. There was a shortbread cookie on the tray, spread with raspberry jam. It looked as if it might be from DiCamillo's Bakery downtown.

Johannes stood up. He went to the stackable cobalt-blue metal-mesh letter trays inherited from the previous math teacher left up-time by the Ring of Fire. He'd cleverly repurposed *her* trays for collecting student work. He had long since divided the trays by class period, as that worked best. The papers for the first period were in the top tray. He flipped through those quickly, looking for missing names, glancing at their work and at the grades. He went through the rest of the class periods. It took a minute, maybe two. No one's grades appeared to have dropped.

Sometimes he felt like he knew the previous teacher through her lesson plans left in the file cabinet. Her graceful handwritten notes on the margins of the teacher's copy of the textbook evoked something in his heart. She was a smart woman. Knew math and loved it. From the picture album—photographs—hidden in a drawer of what was now his desk but had been hers, she'd been pretty, with keen blue eyes and golden-brown hair. From the appellation "Miss," not married at thirty-one, lived and left up-time in a place called Fairmont in West Virginia. He could never meet her but he could teach her classes just as well because of her, and he sort of loved her for that, maybe.

For a moment he thought, *I am so like a shipwrecked soul on a foreign shore! There is no intimacy of any kind in my life. I wish I could meet a woman like her.* He pulled the picture album out and found the lost-in-the-up-time teacher's picture. He blinked. That boy…Timotheus had the same blue eyes and golden hair as she'd had, even. Curious.

There were sirens in the distance, followed by others. Distracted, he put the picture album away. *I really don't want to know what the alarm is for,* he thought and then went back to his papers. He started to grade those, preoccupied for a time with the idea of the teacher lost up-time. He checked off a number of papers in what seemed only a little time.

The Emergency Room, Leahy Medical
About 4:15 p.m., Monday, February 2, 1637

Nurse Dorothea Bayern stood behind the admission desk, catching up on filing patient charts, moving, stooping, standing, rushing. At the moment she had a phone receiver tucked between chin and shoulder and was saying, *"Ja, ja, auf jeden Fall, der Termin ist am Freitag um 10:30 Uhr,"* pausing, listening again, and repeating. This was the sixth telephone call from the same people. "Bitte," Dorothea bit back her annoyance and hung up. *It's not my fault that my accent is weird to them. They said it every single call. So rude.*

Today was fairly quiet. Her main, unwritten, job was that of keeping things moving in Leahy's tiny emergency room during her shift. This day, her shift began at 10:00 a.m. and was supposed to end at 6:00 p.m. In some ways, it didn't seem like it might end at all. It was a good shift to have, since it made her life easier when picking up her daughter from her school's aftercare. Dorothea's mind snapped back to work.

Just a couple of hours before, Dorothea had given wound-care instructions to a young woman who worked in a nearby restaurant just to the west. It had been a simple but deep slice in her hand, between the woman's thumb and her forefinger. Simple but stupid, from some food preparation accident, as the young woman named Brigetta...whatever her surname was...said. "Hey, Charlotte de Lassy! Chary! Give me a hand!"

Chary moved quickly.

"Chary, watch, our patient Brigetta wants minimal scarring and full movement. See, this is how."

"Yes, Dorothea. It's like the best embroidery." Dorothea took care of Brigetta's stitches. Chary watched her to learn the technique.

"That's totally relatable," said Chary.

"Thanks. So do you prefer your Christian name or Chary?"

"Call me Chary," she said, "all the up-timers do."

All kinds of noises drifted into the emergency room through the open, luxurious, perfectly clear, smooth up-time-made glass doors. "Hey, why are those doors open?" Tonight there was a cold breeze rushing in.

Dorothea heard a steady popping like fireworks. Frightened neighing came from several horses just outside, and a man's gravelly voice soothed. All of the noise came from the west on Route 250.

She glanced up from the paperwork, stared through open glass doors, frowned. "Why are those open, Rudy?"

Rudy looked over to her. "I was just out," he admitted.

She sighed. There was that noise. "Did you hear that?" The sound was off, but she couldn't put her finger on why.

"That noise?" Rudy said, "Yeah, not much. Just fireworks or somethin'."

"That house, just down the street..." Dorothea trailed off. *That* house was a good walk away really just to get to the driveway. Dr. von Herbert was having it renovated. Tonight, with the breeze pushing from the northwest and the storm clouds piling snow, sound carried. The hill behind that house probably helped bounce the sound on. It was not actually that loud.

"You want me to walk over?" Rudy asked.

"No, no, I'm sure it's fine," Dorothea said.

Chary stalked over to the admission desk. She looked out the glass doors. "I'm going outside, Doro," she said. "I keep hearing stuff. I was out the back door of the old church and heard the popping, really loud. I'll be careful."

"You'd better be, Chary," Dorothea said. "It's icy out there."

"It'll be fine. I'll just peek and see what's what." Chary shrugged. "And if there are some drunks, I'll tell them to go home. They shouldn't be out in this weather. Too cold for that kind of nonsense."

"Okay. But who would be drunk at this hour?"

"People do strange things around holidays. It's Candlemas." Chary went out into the cold.

Dorothea looked after Chary's determined stride to outside. *Candlemas? That's a Catholic holiday. Isn't it supposed to be somber?*

In a few moments the muffled sounds quit.

Dorothea went to work behind the admission desk managing peoples' schedules. She looked over the tick sheet, added needs to the supply lists, did chart notations, and answered the phone twice in three minutes. When not doing any of those things, she filed, inventoried the supply cabinets, or cared for a patient. Sometimes she'd be shadowed by a new doctor or nurse.

It had been five minutes, then eight. Chary was not yet back.

"Has Chary come back? It's been almost ten minutes. Can you see what's keeping her?" Dorothea asked Dennis. He was one of her orderlies who'd been busy carting supplies down to the main wing's storage room.

"She's outside?" Dennis didn't wait for her answer, just threw on his cloak and went out, slipping on the ice just outside the door, regaining his footing while moving out of sight. The door closed behind him.

Dorothea couldn't remember whether Chary had put her cloak on before she went outside. She didn't know why it was bothering her. Not wearing a cloak outside for a short period of time wouldn't be a terrible thing. She was ten or so years younger than Dorothea. Young enough to be a sister, not a child.

She glanced at the clock. Eleven minutes now since Chary went out.

The outside noises started again. Closer, maybe? Louder. The next sound was a gun shooting very near.

Dorothea jumped. Her pen had jumped across the page, too. She didn't care about that. She looked at the closed glass doors. A rock formed in the pit of her stomach. She hoped she heard wrong.

Dorothea got up from behind the admission desk, hurried to the door, and opened it. She flinched away. That was definitely a gunshot, close maybe. A series of them. She breathed in, then out. She stepped out, cautiously, and looked towards the road. Someone screamed in the distance. If there were any words, she couldn't understand them.

Like Magdeburg, as she remembered. She felt cold all over. Dorothea swallowed. Those last days before running started to dance in her memory.

She pushed them away. Ghosts wouldn't help her now. She reached for the phone and dialed the police.

"Leahy, we're hearing shooting."

The voice on the other end said, "10-4."

She clicked off.

Dennis and Chary came out of the darkness beyond the entrance lights. Chary's face was pale, her white and gray and blue uniform dark and shining wet. No cloak. Between them they dragged someone wearing a maid's cap. The white cap was askew.

Dorothea glanced up. Chary and Dennis had almost made it to the ER doors before Chary nearly dropped the woman. Dorothea looked back. Rudy rushed across the lobby with a gurney.

Time slowed.

Dorothea hit her little radio's call button. "Doctor Adams, to the ER, please!"

On a typical day, Dorothea would have one doctor or another in the ER or on a radio but in the building. Sometimes she'd have a good dozen, other times, like today, three. Few of the little radios remained in Leahy. Dorothea did not actually care about the radios. They were a convenience she'd gotten used to.

Batteries, she thought, *has that been taken care of? When was the last order?*

"Sorry," Chary gasped out.

"It's fine. You got her to me," Dennis said. He managed to turn his grip on the maid into a bridal carry, bringing her into the ER. Leaving a trail of blood drops behind, he placed her on the gurney.

Finally the radio hissed, "10-4, Doro, what've ya got? I'm five minutes away. Just leaving the PLC."

"Gunshot wound, at least one. Neck, shoulder, arm, check her abdominals, there's a hole in the dress."

"10-4, as fast as I can. Get 'er prepped! Call in the others."

"Understood, Dr. Adams." Dorothea clicked off that channel, called the others, then clipped her radio back to her belt. She went to Chary.

A moment later, sirens blared from the east. From the sound, close to the parking lot.

"You okay?" Dorothea grabbed Chary's cold hand, pulled her up and back onto her feet.

"I don't think I've run so fast on ice in my life." Chary winced, still gasping.

They walked into the ER together, slowly. Chary sniffled. "I hurt!" She leaned against a wall.

Dr. Adams arrived, tossed his coat over the nearest desk, grabbed the end of the gurney that the maid was loaded on, and leaned in to examine. Dorothea noted in a glance that the maid's upper shoulder had at least two bullet holes in it, along with a neck wound, bruised eye swollen shut, arm broken, wrist broken, like she'd been beaten, then shot. Dr. Adams swore a streak, before bellowing, "Dido Besen! Get here! Rudy, get here!"

Dido materialized next to him. She was always a presence of calm, her black braids already pulled back, capped, gowned, and scrubbed, ready to rescrub and glove.

Rudy was close behind, gowned, too.

"Pressure here. Now. We've got to stanch this. Examine for other wounds. Rudy, move it! Move! Move! Surgery!"

The door to Surgery 1 swung shut firmly behind them. There was work to do. The anesthesiologist, an older man, Herr Böhm, went through the door, shoving them open. His voice rang out as he did. "But there is no other way to do this! I can care for my Anna, my niece, without losing my head!"

The door closed before Doctor Adams replied. His voice was muffled. Herr Böhm's response was even quieter; the only distinct word was "family."

As Dorothea and Chary passed the admission desk, Dennis called the nursing office at the tech college for backup per the plan.

Today there was a Professional Learning Community training at the tech college on specific surgeries for emergency room patients. The training had run all day. Dorothea thought, *I was on that list to go! My relief, Sabine Reuter, is at home tending to a sick husband.* Otherwise, she would've left at 2:00 p.m. to attend the PLC's afternoon session. Dorothea had the worst feeling that all the preparation in the world would be nothing in the face of chaos that was coming to stir and stir and stir a mess dragging into the ER. She closed her eyes to make a silent prayer for strength, before she remembered. *Oh, no—Arabella! Who's getting her from the aftercare at school?* She reached for the phone to call Frau Böhm on the high school's cafeteria extension.

Chary slowly sat down in a nearby chair. Before Dorothea could leave her and go back to the admission desk, Chary grabbed her wrist. Her breathing was shaky, scared. Tears dripped down her pale face. "I think I got hit, Doro."

Another nurse, Barbie Schmidt, who'd just arrived, was already by Chary's side. "Let me see," she said gently. She took Chary back to a screened-off section.

Two men came in. Dorothea recognized the one in the EMT uniform. The other wore ordinary clothes and was vaguely familiar.

A green truck sped by from the east blaring sirens so loud you could hear it clearly through the doors. She blinked. The sameness of noise day after day tricked her, lulled her into its ordinariness. *How could I be so complacent, so stupid?* Dorothea thought, angry with herself. The sounds were normal. That was a mistake. *This place is safe.*

The housekeeper from the von Herberts' was standing in front of the admission desk. Someone must have brought her. She recognized the woman, but couldn't remember her name. Was her name...Frau Hummel? She'd come once with *that girl* on one of her bad pain days...Magdalena Vogel? The older woman swayed, bleeding, looking grayer by the second. Dorothea yelled for Dennis. Between the two of them, they got her on the gurney and started the prep. The stanching of the wounds in her side did not really seem to work, so she was rushed into the second surgery room. This patient seemed to whisper to the EMTs.

Two in surgery. Both surgeries were occupied at this point.

The clock ticked loudly for two minutes. Time seemed as if it was in a sort of syrupy stop, trickling by.

A pale, bleeding young man arrived, a workman from the von Herbert house down the road. "I got away! I got away! They're all dead there!" he sobbed out in agony. His forearm was broken by a bullet, bent weirdly and the skin partially unsleeved, exposing the muscles beneath. He cried, tears running down his cheeks, gasping, "This wound, can you fix me?" Someone dragged him to the hallway and started working on him.

A good dozen nurses and doctors arrived from the PLC. Someone pushed a cart with bottles of typed blood towards the surgeries.

Some poor workman bled out, time called, the floor slickly wet with his blood. One of his hands was missing all the fingers. He was packed up to be carted to the morgue. Another workman was brought in, immediately called, then carted to the morgue. Nothing could be done. A third workman, also.

Chaos was dancing its little jig. Panic trailed her, but Dorothea wouldn't let it take her. Not yet. There was too much to do.

Another horse cart pulled in.

Herr Johannes Esslie's Math Classroom, Grantville High School
After School, February 2, 1637

Johannes Esslie walked over to his classroom window, leaned out, and glanced downstairs. The fire engine sirens were right there. The big red fire truck pulled in, right up to the high school to turn it around. He could just see it out of his classroom window; the angle was awkward. The crackle of what he'd thought might be fireworks was more rhythmic. That came from the west. Johannes blinked the spots from his eyes, thinking, *I've ridden this horse more than once—never again!* He walked away from the window.

Johannes turned, catching his appearance in the mirror hanging on the wall opposite the window. The mirror was also inherited from the math teacher from the up-time. The mirror said everything about her, its elaborate Venetian style, beveled edges and all with the flair and floral etching on the mirrored frame. It was not a big mirror. She must have had money.

Above the mirror was a little wooden sign in a playful font: *"Hello, Gorgeous!"*

His reasoning always led to the idea that this teacher had been a wit.

In the mirror Johannes appeared tall and spindly. His eyes were worried, cheeks hollowed, the scraggly beard just touched with the first sign of gray in its brown, badly pointed end. So unhealthy. He was as pale as the snow outside. Not in the least gorgeous.

The months of *his* illness had taken his health, which had never been robust, but had been adequate. He missed feeling as healthy as he had last September, last October. That's when he started feeling a little tired no matter how much sleep he'd had, and he'd had no idea what misery was to come. Dear God in Heaven, the constant coughing started in so small a way. Just little coughs. It wasn't tuberculosis, according to the doctors. They tested for it several times, months apart, just in case. *Dr. von Herbert said that the plague would have finished me already.* No one seemed to know what this illness was. He did not want to think about it, but could not escape it. But two weeks ago, the doctor thought it might be a lingering pneumonia and gave him antibiotics.

Johannes shook his head as he went back to his desk. He coughed again. Not as deep as before, but it still left him gasping and holding his ribs. The room was starting to feel cold, but he didn't want to close up just yet.

Another siren sounded, much closer, as the vehicle raced by the school from the east, then disappeared as it got too far away, closer to town. The silence outside which followed was sharp and brief. A fire engine sped by the school, its siren wail reverberating. It must have been on some other call. Both vehicles were of up-time construction. Johannes drank some of the hot tea. As always, his throat felt raw. That first sip of tea always felt terrible going down. He winced and made himself sip again. The next one felt better.

He started the checklist and ran over it for a few minutes, considering his dilemma. *I've set up for the math test tomorrow. Rothrock can handle that. It's not like our department chair, Herr Fleming, or even Master Oughtred, can be everywhere! I've already been to the copy center, picked those sets up.*

There was a loud bang from the stairs at the end of the hall. Something metal clattered. Then came the loud tap-tap of hard-soled boots coming closer, running. Almost immediately, the classroom door shook from someone violently hammering on it. Johannes got up out of his wheeled rolling chair and went towards the door. Before he got to it, a key turned in the lock, and the door was shoved open. It twanged the metal stopper.

Johannes stepped backwards. "You know you could be more patient. I was coming!"

James Rothrock rushed in. He stood there for a moment, breathing hard. He'd just run up twenty-five stairs. He said, "Esslie! Are you set? Are we set?" Rothrock's voice was loud, adolescent even, not that of a man in his early thirties. "Leahy needs paramedics. They need extra hands. We already have the tech center nursing students coming! There's been an incident at the von Herberts'."

"What? What? Incident, where?" Johannes felt the blood leave his face. Something inside made him flinch. He'd not been all that involved for some time. He still remembered enough though. "Put that back in order, James. Please."

"You've heard the sirens?"

"Of course!" Johannes hoped he was wrong. "For the last, I don't know, fifteen minutes, twenty minutes, or so. And thundering, fireworks. It's not thunder or fireworks?"

"Ha! Hell, no! No, it's snowing out, and it's not thunder snow! Besides, it's Candlemas. If you're Catholic!" Rothrock said. Vibrating from tension, pale.

"I'm not. No." Johannes glared. "I'm not going there. What happened? You're...grim." He trembled as if he were more ill than what was now his normal state.

Rothrock didn't notice *that* tremble. "Damn right. On the radio, the up-timers called it a home invasion. Big city stuff, for them. It's, it's bleak! Near Leahy. Amalia von Herbert and Maggie Vogel are not accounted for. My girl, Anna! I was at your place to drop off a box of work, tests, hell, the gradebook—you weren't expected today. The von Herberts' down the street! Got called! We need everybody."

"No. I don't want to. I'm too damn sick!"

Rothrock said. He held a hand up. "I know. You're sick as a dead cow. You're not dying."

Finally Esslie got out, "You went to my place without asking me? So I come with you, whether I'm up for it or not?" Johannes went and closed the windows.

"Yes, we thought you'd be there. The school didn't know if you were there, here, on your way, or sitting in a bar getting drunk."

"I don't drink to get drunk! I was supposed to be at Leahy for an appointment."

Rothrock's voice was firm. "You didn't go? Why?"

"I feel better," Johannes said, excusing it, exhaling. Looked away.

"Money, again? You're better than you were. You're not a spendthrift. You're a damn good shot. You can shoot and help organize. Leahy will pay you for that."

"I don't need...charity."

"As it was, your landlady let me in. I dropped the papers and grade book off on your...table. I've brought your pistol, the kit. I'm carrying a radio so I got the call. No, you're not donating blood. What the hell is that map on your wall, anyway?"

Johannes protested, thinking, *this is horrifying,* "Shoot at what? You know I'm out of that game, yes? My landlady let you into my room? My room at the boarding house on the river? You saw the map?"

Rothrock nodded. "The map. Lots of strings and arrows and red Xs on that wall. Names, places, events. What the hell, man! That was a climb up. The stairs in the Netherlands are worse but not by much, Johannes. Those stairs at your place, man! So damn narrow. How do you manage it? It's so steep. Just the wrong step, and you fall over the edge into that *wirtschaft*."

"Alright, I am still limber, and it is not my heart which is the problem." Johannes reflected, *my room!* There was a bed cupboard on one side, a fireplace on the other. The glass window wrinkled into a corner, overlooking the river. The view was nice. His room was relatively warm, the rent was cheap, meals cost him little. And, for now, it was home. He wondered, *how did Rothrock get there and back so quickly?*

"I left a while back as I was dropping your mess of papers and such off. Then we were called. I heard it and came here. The von Herbert neighbors evacuated before the *thing* started. A lot of people have been called in. Time is wasting!"

Johannes, exploding, shouted, "Why the hell would Frau Heinlein let you in? What do you know?"

"Frau Heinlein let me in. I showed her the note from Ditmar Schaub! She wouldn't do it until then—your friend from NESS is crazy. What the hell is that about?"

Johannes sighed. "It's...not much."

Rothrock opened the classroom door. "We gotta go!" He turned and looked back at Johannes, apparently not satisfied. "What the hell was that big map on your wall with all the markers? Explain."

"I'm tracing something important, James." Johannes pulled on his coat and gloves.

Rothrock gave him a sideways glance. "For the CoC?"

"The von Herbert girl and the Vogel girl? And your girlfriend? Their names are up there, too." Johannes' heart sank, his stomach was flipping. He picked up the lunch container and thermos off his desk, and followed Rothrock out of the room. He dropped the thermos and lunch container on the janitor's cart as he passed it. "Has anyone heard—"

"No one knows anything!" Rothrock interrupted.

They moved quickly. Rothrock was fast ahead of him. Johannes coughed some more, spat into his handkerchief. *"Oh mein Gott! Und wir sind unwissend?"*

"God bless it! You're not tubercular, Esslie! It's not fucking bloody! We need to hurry!"

Johannes made his way, slowly, to the top step of the stairs. Rothrock waited impatiently at the bottom. Johannes coughed, hacked up another clot of grimy mucus, and breathed heavily.

"I cannot hurry! I hate this sickness." Johannes gasped out as he walked down the stairs.

"I hope so. I hope it's only that, and not a whooping cough," Rothrock said.

Johannes sighed. Not knowing what it was was terrible.

The heavy metal door in the stairwell to the outside of the high school slammed behind them, leaving them in the rotten cold wind. It was one of the back doors.

He asked, "We're footing it?"

James Rothrock gave him that look.

Johannes exhaled. "What the hell."

Route 250
Sometime After 5:00 p.m., February 2, 1637

The horses pulled the gray and green cart easily along the snowy, icy road. The jingle of the bells bound to red-stained leather harnesses was cheerful. The cart's pair of lanterns near the front swayed slightly with the breeze and the jiggle of the horses.

A blast sounded, followed by a rumble, and then a sense of air rushing.

Young Fred shouted, "Grandpa, do you see that man, in the trees, up that driveway?"

Someone was shooting. Old Fred thought about it. *Guns. I'm a gunsmith, used to be, haven't been for a while. Each type has its own sound, its own feel.* "This is crazy," he said, "why are they shooting? What are they shooting? It's a musket. No, I think it is a caliver."

"Sounds like it, Grandpa, it's close! Isn't this the driveway to the house where Anna works?" Young Fred asked.

There were several cars rushing up from behind. Those emergency lights flashed violently.

Old Fred glanced back at the driveway, nickering at the horses. "Maybe. We need to get outta here."

A pair of *fräuleins* ran out from just where the tree-covered hill hit State Route 250, waving at him. Well, one was trying to wave while she dragged the other along. Neither was dressed for the weather.

Young Fred cried out, "Stop, grandpa! We need to save them!"

More shots. Six, no, eight. Old Fred exclaimed, "There's three guns in play here!"

"This isn't Magdeburg, Grandpa!"

More shots. "They're shooting at us! Hurry!" Old Fred nickered to his horses, holding them firm. Something pinched him on his right side, twice. Young Fred leaped out of the cart, dragged the young *fräuleins* into the cart as quick as a light switch flicked on in a dark room. He lifted the smaller one first into the back of the cart, then the taller one rolled in, and Young Fred clambered in.

Old Fred drove his horse cart towards the ER at Leahy as fast as the horse could manage without slipping, yelling back. "Freddie! Freddie, hang on! Hold on to them!" *I hurt,* Old Fred thought.

"Yes, Grandpa!" Young Fred called out.

Twilight had already turned to dusk. Night was running over the whole landscape, skeletonizing the already winter-barren trees. In three minutes, they arrived at Leahy Medical, pulled up to the ER. Old Fred made certain they were far enough along that the cart wasn't blocking everything, but close enough. Modern technology was sometimes almost magic. He knew it wasn't but, still.

Old Fred noted a few armed men nearby a dozen paces away, seemingly guarding the hospital. NESS came to mind then left his thoughts entirely. He climbed out and down from the cart. His side pinched hard. He felt light-headed. Breathing painfully, he gingerly walked the icy pavement 'round to the back of the cart.

Young Fred rolled out of the cart from where he'd been holding the two *fräuleins*. The boy was bloody. He slipped and slid his way across the dozen yards to the ER yelling in up-time English. Old Fred hoped his situation was better than it seemed.

Old Fred traced the bullet holes in the side of his horse cart that had faced von Herbert's home. He looked back, saw the flicker of the police car lights. "Hm." *My side hurts, damn. I didn't know it was this many! They hit too low to kill us. If I didn't know better, those would be, what, warning shots? Like at Magdeburg?* Old Fred had visions of throwing Young Fred and Anna in the back of a smaller horse cart. Of a house collapsed, of fires and bodies everywhere. Old Fred exhaled, dropped the rear gate to this horse cart. *It'll make it a bit easier getting them both out.*

He breathed out streaming a thin fog. *It hurt!* All this excitement wasn't good for him. He made his way back to the front of the horse cart, and heard one of the *fräuleins* sobbing. He told her, as calmly as he could, "We got here! I can't do anything more, *liebchen*. I'm sorry I can't."

The girl sniffled, prayed in Latin.

"Yes, *liebchen*." Old Fred reached over and patted her arm. Her tears stopped for a moment. He thought her name was Maggie, Magdelena. Young Fred always talked of her. They'd survived the siege of Magdeburg in May of 1631, in the safety of the Premonstratensian Monastery. Old Fred exhaled. His older daughter was dragged out screaming by wicked soldiers. He could still hear her screams. Maggie stared at him for just a moment, before she melted down again.

He heard Young Fred yelling in Amideutsch since the English hadn't gotten them moving—from inside the emergency room entryway. The doors were wide open, but he couldn't see inside. How many were in there? How bad was it?

"Amalia! Please wake up!" Maggie's voice broke as she wept

Medical people swarmed Old Fred's horse cart. Some young men, very strong and experienced with horses from the look, grabbed the harnesses and held the four horses steady. The good steeds twitched nervously, snorted, and tapped their feet. Old Fred nickered at them gently. Afterwards they seemed preternaturally calm. From the size and apparent ages, they weren't warhorses, at least not now, but seemed to remember what to do.

Someone pulled Old Fred away, distracting him for a moment, looked him over, and began to pat him, focused on his side, the side that had been towards *that* house.

The inspection did not amuse nor concern him. He thought, *I am going to stay home for at least a week. I'm too old for this misadventure!*

Old Fred watched as the other medical staff climbed into the cart to get to his passengers. The medical staff pulled Maggie away, got her to let go. Maggie's hands were red and slick. Red splattered across her front, up her forearms, speckled across her face and neck, everywhere. Blood. Maggie was a horror in this bright light but she slowly walked into the ER on her own, sobbing, with an orderly alongside her.

Thankfully, it seemed she still had the sense to not put her face into her hands.

The one identified by Maggie as Amalia was blood-soaked and so pale she could've been dead. Old Fred had seen too many corpses in his time that looked better than her. He hoped, prayerfully, something could be done.

Old Fred allowed himself to be led away towards the hospital's emergency room. He complained in mumbles.

An orderly and an RN supported him, explaining how he needed to be checked over. He was assured by them that his *pretty steeds* would be well looked after. Old Fred glanced back to the parking lot. In that short distance several of the young men had the horses in hand, still hooked up to the cart, and were leading them to the stable just up the driveway.

He looked towards his right. The last he saw of Amalia that night, she was loaded on a gurney with a nurse on top doing what the up-timers called CPR and another rushing alongside holding a bottle filled with some kind of clear liquid. Two orderlies kept everything steady.

He walked a few steps into the emergency room, no more than five or six. His legs wouldn't hold him anymore. He dropped to the ground. The pain in his chest and side thundered. His eyes felt heavy. He looked up at the dusking sky through the outside doors, swallowed into the darkness.

The last thing Old Fred heard for a very long time was Young Fred yelling, "Grandpa!"

Emergency Room, Leahy Medical Center
About 5:25 p.m., February 2, 1637

Dorothea barely noticed the collapse of the old man halfway through the propped-open doors. He dropped like a tree, grabbing at his chest, his clothes bloody. The people with him tried to catch him on the way down, but the fall was too fast. His head hit the floor. Dorothea only knew because she was close to the ER door and heard it. She winced. The man's head hitting the floor was most definitely a concussion. Dr. Adams saw the entire sequence. He peeled off his bloody apron, threw it aside, accepted a fresh one from an orderly, and rushed over.

Dorothea gingerly stepped through the crowded room to her next patient, careful of the slick blood on the floor, careful not to bump into anyone. Her skirt hit just below mid-calf, so she wasn't trailing blood but her boots would never be the same. Had she worn her espadrilles, it would have been worse.

Dorothea looked over to where an orderly was mopping the blood and melting ice and called out to him. "Dennis, here, now!"

"Yes, ma'am!"

Dorothea barely heard him over the noise. Screaming, crying, begging, as her nursing team moved with purpose to do what they could. Identifying one man was just impossible. His facial wounds were that terrible. And if he survived long enough for surgery... She did not want to think of that, if the patient made it that far. She looked up when she heard her name shouted by two different people with two different gurneys.

"Where can we put these patients!"

"Hallway, again!" Dorothea pointed out the direction. "Stick with them! I've got someone here!"

Her patient was a man who had a bullet wound in his hip. It looked to have been the result of a high-caliber weapon. Some of his fingers were broken and bent wrong, but she didn't bother touching them. Too swollen. His shattered jaw and cheekbone were not wounded in precisely the same way. A large, narrow blunt object must have done it, and perhaps used more than once. Blood pooled underneath the skin making it look deep bluish-purple, swelling up half of his face. Somehow, Dorothea had to figure out how to prepare him as next in line and give him opium to reduce the pain in just the right way. He was taken out of her hands, away to surgery.

Dorothea glanced over the admission desk and noted that a man had taken it over. She wasn't sure of his name, perhaps Wolfram Kuntz. He'd leaned in to speak to a man who had a yellow scarf wrapped around his neck and sort of covering his mouth. The other man looked sickly greenish in the light. He'd taken over from Rudy Piepmatz, freeing him up for other things, and it looked like he was being replaced in turn.

She looked across the emergency room. The up-timers called this sort of mass care "triage" in every PLC training they did on patient care; she'd been in dozens of training sessions. Dorothea had practiced it that awful day in 1635 when the demonstration outside the hospital had turned into a deadly riot. Triage was a method to contain the madness, sorting patients by the severity of their conditions, making an order out of chaos. Triage improved survival. Sorting out the worst injured people was an art. Some of those wounded were sent immediately to surgery, either one of the two ORs or other spaces set up in haste. Others had their wounds dressed in the ER cubicles, then had been sent to Outpatient. The level-two low-needs patients were being treated in the closer hallways. The dead were taken directly to the morgue across the parking lot.

More injured trickled in. Two in surgery, four in the beds, six in chairs in the hall. Some were not physically hurt, but perhaps in shock, especially those scared in the mind by horrendous things. There was a sorting clinic in a tent outside. Even Dorothea, as the current shift's head, didn't know how many people were there. She'd find out later. It seemed like an endless line of wounded people. In two cases—no, three—bodies, obviously murdered in firing squad-style. Dorothea sent those to the morgue, felt the tears start, and did her best to shove those aside. She did not want to become inhuman. But tears wouldn't help anyone right now.

Six dead, so far. She looked at the clock, which read almost 5:30 pm. *Tempus fugit! A minute ago it'd been 5:15...maybe? Where was Barbara Schmidt?*

As far as Dorothea could figure out, someone had taken refuge in the rising hills and woods behind those houses down the road. That person decided to start shooting randomly at everyone. There was nothing she could do except what she was already doing, and she hoped that there wasn't another wave of patients. She moved on to her next patient, trying to push her feelings down, away.

Emergency Room, Leahy Medical Center
About 5:30 p.m., February 2, 1637

Dorothea noticed Rudy was on a gurney pushed by two orderlies, performing the CPR, kneeling over a bloody young man, chanting, "Stayin' alive! Live, live, live! Stayin' alive!" to keep in rhythm. She could hear the lost-to-up-time Bee Gees wailing that musical tune in her head. She then remembered that this coming weekend was a disco night at the high school, a dance they called it, and instantly felt guilty over the very thought.

A few minutes later Dr. Adams came out of surgery, wiping his hands. He opened his mouth to speak and was cut off by an explosion coming from the direction of Buffalo Creek. The windows vibrated. The whole building shook. Dorothea looked back, but Dr. Adams was out of sight. The surgery's door was shut. It was like he'd never been there. The clock ticked. She noticed a hairline crack in one of the perfect glass doors at the upper corner.

The rumble of another boom rolled through, shaking the hospital. Worse, it was closer. The crack in the glass door spiderwebbed.

The emergency room doors were wide open to the winter wind. Snow swirled in glittering dots lit up by the parking lot lights. The police outside in the brewing storm were on high alert.

A shriek of terror blasted into the emergency room from outside. Dorothea ran to the open door, yelling, "Simon, Jacobs! What happened?"

The gurney wobbled to a stop. Both of her orderlies struggled to keep the gurney upright. The young woman on the gurney had no vitals in triage just moments before when Dorothea called the time of *that* death.

One of the orderlies, Simon, yelled back while holding the gurney steady. "She sat up, Nurse! When the bomb went off! She's not dead! She's screaming!"

The other orderly was trying to soothe the young woman, whispering to her.

Dorothea stared. "What!?" She could see the figure struggling to sit up and not able to. "Simon, Jacobs! Get her back in here! "

"She's supposed to be dead! How can she be alive?" Jacobs yelled back, holding the gurney still.

"Get her back in here! Now!" Dorothea yelled.

"But, but, but..."

"Now!"

"But she's dead!" Jacobs looked so confused.

"And now she's not!" Simon yelled back, tugging on the gurney. "Let's keep her that way!"

The originally inert young shape pushed up against the restraints again and again, struggling. Her eyes blinked furiously, mouth open and screaming and trying to catch her breath as if she was drowning. After a short time an odd sort of gasping noise came out of her mouth, and she lay down, wheezing. A small drip of blood rolled down her face from a head wound.

Simon gently rolled her on her side, restrapped. Her breathing settled. The gurney got shoved back into the ER, anyway, Simons arguing with Jacobs. About undeads, *whatever that was.*

The blood-soaked young woman had been dead. No doubts. On review, Amalia was faintly pink, gasping, somehow awakened on the edge of life. So young. *The von Herberts would've cracked*, Dorothea thought, *might still if we cannot do anything.* She prayed silently in thanks that she would not have to tell them.

Tears started to drip down Dorothea's face. She sniffled, wiped her eyes with her sleeve. Breathed deep. Disaster averted. *Faith manages,* she thought, twisting her tiny gold hamsa hand on its little chain, then tucked it away.

The EMT who had worked on the young woman's body was vaguely familiar to Dorothea. Until he saw the young woman wheeled back in, he was sweating blood, terrified. It took a moment to remember his name. *Rothrock.* Not important enough. *I never speak to him, ever.* Something had happened a long time before... the Villareals? There were things about the summer of 1634, *something* terrible had happened. A murder, an assault, an arrest, a trial, a hanging. Rothrock was rotten slime, hardly human. They didn't hang him then, fine line, there. She turned over in her mind, *Rothrock is an EMT. Not a diseased maniac. So useful since...Stop distracting yourself!*

Dorothea's attention snapped elsewhere. There were two more workmen from von Herbert's backyard, severely wounded, gunshot. She went over to help Dr. Adams with one of them, skidded on a patch of blood, caught herself, managing to stay upright.

Dr. Adams looked over at her and said, "Watch it. You *cannot* get hurt. Sew this up for me. Where'd they stick the live-wire?"

"Yes, Doctor. Needle? They put her in the OR just cleaned."

"Yes, good. Use the black silk. It's finer. Hurry!" Dr. Adams moved off quickly, yelling, as he dumped his blood-soaked apron and thin leather gloves in the bin, grabbing another, this new apron stained but clean. "Scrub it up, folks! Let's roll!"

Two nurses who'd only just arrived followed, as did others.

Dorothea did the sew-up on the workman, closing the flesh delicately in tiny firm stitches as the rest was already done. Bullets removed, dumped in an evidence tray. The man she was working on would live.

Barely awake, the man asked her, "Do you believe in God, Nurse? Some of the Grantvillers don't seem to think of Him."

Dorothea blinked, stopped for a moment, replied softly, "I think in medicine, as in anything, faith manages." She finished sewing the man's thigh, spreading raw honey over the long wound's neatly stitched edges, then bandaged him.

He nodded and closed his eyes. "I am so tired, *Fräulein*. Do you see that tiny box over there?"

She nodded, a raised eyebrow, said softly, "You need to stay at least overnight, perhaps two nights." Dorothea glanced at his name-tag. "You lost blood but not enough to warrant a transfusion, Herr Nachtnebelwald. Do you want me to hand you the little box? I'm"—she glanced around, said softly—"clean."

"Ah, yes," he murmured, nodded, relieved.

She passed him the little prayer box. Dorothea got up, whispered to an orderly who brought a wheeled chair. "I'm having you taken to recovery. The doctor there will decide how long you need to stay here."

"Thank you, thank you." He was helped into the wheeled chair. The little box went with him.

Dorothea said to him, in careful German, "*Sie sind herzlich willkommen. Bitte sagen sie der Krankenschwester im Aufwachraum Bescheid, wenn sie Schmerzen haben oder sich unwohl fühlen.*"

He nodded. Didn't remark on her accent, which was complicated enough with all the blending of languages in her head. So he must have understood her well enough. It was interesting that he was of similar origin to her; she didn't hear Hochdeutsch like this man's very often. And hiding, even in the safety of Grantville.

An information pack for the patient was stuck in a pouch attached to the chair. The orderly pushed the chair off down the hall, whistling, of all things.

Someone ran into the ER and loudly announced that someone from CSI was coming from the von Herbert house.

Dorothea looked up to see a figure stride through the emergency room as if it were not filled with people. He was not from *die polizei*. She knew his face. He came straight at her. Stopped.

"Show me," he demanded, like a king, maybe.

"You saw?" She made herself ask.

He nodded once.

"Yes. This way," Dorothea responded.

For a moment all was still as a pane of glass. She didn't know if anyone noticed what just occurred. Most were too busy trying not to die or were too busy keeping people from dying, she supposed.

Another terrific boom from the direction of Buffalo Creek rolled over. It was the third boom in less than twenty minutes. Dorothea's nerves danced again. *It was like the boom of a cannon.* A man's scream was cut off. She hoped he was unconscious.

The tall aristocratic man followed her. Dorothea guided him to the surgery and noticed the height again. It wasn't just fancy boots. He dropped his cloak, jacket, and hat on a random side table, changed to the surgery booties, clipped his hair back, scrubbed, gowned with the apron and gloved up. He said with supernatural calm, "Now you have another surgeon. My wife and son have gone to the sunroom in the Women and Children's wing. My wife is certain to donate blood."

"Thank you, yes, Doctor." Dorothea nodded and returned to the ER.

His facial expression was distant, maybe a little cold, but his eyes were blazing. They were the same color as his daughter's. Dorothea hoped that Amalia wouldn't die under his hands. She hoped Dr. Adams would attend.

After she changed her apron, several more nurses arrived, carrying bags of gear, apparently from the up-time fire truck that had just pulled into the parking lot, lights flashing. At the admission desk stood Martin Dörren-felde and Fire Chief Matheny. She caught none of what they were saying.

But it didn't help her sense of dread to hear the chatter among the other people in the room. It was all wildly 'in-the-twilight-zone' rumors.

Dorothea exhaled. She didn't know the name of the patient who yelled, almost in her ear. "Truth is unfortunately scarce!"

"It always is," she said.

"This isn't Magdeburg, you know!" the man said.

Dorothea nodded, walked onward. Checked on her nurses, gave help if needed.

Someone else claimed, "There's five dead invaders."

Johannes Esslie, whose name Dorothea finally remembered, working the admission desk after Herr Kuntz stepped away, coughed into his scarf and said, "There's more out there, a dozen or more at least!"

She said to him, "We don't know that yet."

He stared at her like he'd seen a ghost. It was disconcerting. His mouth opened and closed, opened again as if to speak, then didn't.

The flow of patients slowed. The last ones were lightly wounded. And they had stories to tell. A patient claimed this was an act of the devil. Some woman said a dead maid was found with thirty silver coins in her pocket, and that *no one* knew who she was. So she was a traitor. Or a spy. Or worse. Still another talked of a cook and four workmen shot in the basement, then dragged outside to bleed and freeze. Someone else claimed that the so-called dead maid was alive.

But what was finally known was that Dr. von Herbert's house was in the process of being searched, from cellar to attic, all three-thousand-something square feet of it. Its grounds and the neighboring homes were being searched. Even the wooded hills behind the von Herbert house were searched for hiding places. No one had said what was really being looked for. It seemed as if every first responder who could be spared from elsewhere was brought in for the search.

Dorothea considered what she knew. Almost half of the workmen had talked to her about Magdeburg, but that was almost six years in the past. Men deliberately hired because of Magdeburg?

Armed men attacking just one house in Grantville? A doctor's house? It was an uncomfortable open secret that von Herbert was at Magdeburg, but not in the city. It was rumored that he'd stood with Tilly or probably someone else as he hadn't been high up in the *Katholische Liga*. Yet, this happened. *But is it only that?* She hesitated before she approached Fire Chief Matheny and Martin Dörrenfelde. She saw Ditmar Schaub and his men walking towards Route 250. At least that man walked like him. *Am I absolutely certain this was an attempted assassination over a grudge? This is something personal. This is not political. But what if I'm wrong?*

It took a few moments for Dorothea to realize Johannes Esslie was not at the admission desk anymore. *Where'd he go?*

The von Herbert House
Dusk, February 2, 1637

Snow crunched under his feet as Johannes Esslie followed a narrow bloody trail from Leahy Medical to the edge of Route 250 towards the west. The von Herbert house was not far. Twice the trail of blood diverged into three sets of blood-soaked footprints inside the parking lot. Down 250 was a defined trail. He expected it would go up that steep little driveway. In one place, the snow showed where someone had fallen but had gotten up. The weight of his pistol and his rifle were a comfort. He listened to the crackling to the west. Gunshots echoing off the hills. *Chief Richards had to have called Camp Saale. And certainly Her Honor Frau Carstairs was the one behind the sirens. If they're not already here, they will be soon.* He stopped at Route 250, exhaled, considered.

This reminded him of Magdeburg. Of being on the city walls *that* morning, so early, so very early on May 20, 1631. He had been there, as he had been often, in the defensive position shooting a gun—any of several—picking off the careless and passing each empty back to someone not trained well enough to snipe in exchange for a freshly loaded gun. *My attendant died behind me then. Hmm.*

Across Route 250 from the hospital was DiCamillo's Café. He'd not been inside this somewhat-new second location. One of the café windows was spiderwebbed with cracks spreading from a series of bullet holes. The main DiCamillo's Bakery and Café was on Main Street next to Rupert the Butcher's, not too far from *his* gunsmith's.

Johannes missed the baker who'd made the best *spritzkuchen* in Magdeburg or anywhere. Johannes knew they'd not gotten out, as the baker was the type to rebuild somewhere. He exhaled, considering that it was too bad; the baker would be here in Grantville in his new shop, selling pastries like a madman and loving his family with the same intensity and joy if he was still alive, but he was not, and neither was his family. *So many regrets. I couldn't find them even though I looked for a long time.*

Johannes walked out onto Route 250, up the slight rise, doing his best not to slip. The specter of failed negotiation haunted him, of city fathers hunted down, butchered. *My father did what he could. And I did as well as I could.* He'd hidden himself, shoved in a small alley, scraped along it, hiding in a recess between buildings not far from the city gate nearest to the moat going to the Elbe River. The river was not in the spring flood stage, nor was it raging in any way. It was flowing fast enough to make it a possible escape route, though a dangerous one.

So many people got caught running away. He almost got caught a dozen times, shot back twice, and killed once of which he was certain.

Johannes stood at the edge of the highway, in the inconvenient breeze, freezing, boots ankle-deep in almost fresh snow. It was well into dusk. On either side some distance away were a number of other people—police officers, CoC people, NESS even, but he didn't care. *Not my concern,* he decided. Looking down the road, he could see the lights from several torches on that piece of the hill. Some of those were high enough up that they must be inside von Herbert's house. Johannes could almost see how they moved around and through it. *At least the scheißkerl hadn't had the chance to burn it down.*

Even from his distant viewpoint, Johannes saw a few of the windows were gone altogether. *This is the west side. Six hundred feet from here. That raises many questions.*

He glanced back to the hill behind DiCamillo's Café. There were several buildings on the west side of it, one a house almost directly behind the café, which was in some kind of converted building. *I saw something moving. What is that?* Johannes turned slightly to the east to look properly. Skeletal trees clad the hill behind the cafe and several up-time houses, then climbed further into the empty woods behind. The woods were scrubby, nearly bare because it was winter, but those had never actually been lush. *There it is again, a movement. Whose?*

Crunching footsteps came from behind. A sideways glance told him it was one of the men from NESS, and that man was Ditmar Schaub. The bushy beard gave him away.

"I'm thinking," Johannes said to him, still staring at the woods. "What do we know?"

"You're armed?" Schaub asked softly, looking him over, noting his weapons.

Johannes side-eyed him, shrugged. "The usual, my pistol. It's the Sharps pepperbox, up-timer thing. I also have the rifle you see, ammunition. A Bowie knife. A few other things. Rothrock brought my kit." He exhaled. "It is really frustrating. He shouldn't have gone there."

Schaub exhaled. "I see. Does he know?"

"Hell, no. I really do not appreciate you giving him a note to my landlady," Johannes said. "I am not explaining this to Rothrock. He already saw and asked about the map pinned to my wall, so I put him off. Has anyone checked the woods?"

"We've got men up there," Schaub snapped.

Johannes nodded, smirked. The expression felt foreign on his face. He feigned relief. "Oh, good. Do you know what you are hunting?"

"That is a good question. I gather this is not political," Schaub said.

Johannes shook his head. "It's not political. I do not believe it'll slide that way." He paused. "Pains have been taken. So. Do you know what you are hunting? Whom you are hunting?"

The men looked at each other. Johannes felt like his eyes were slicing and dicing Ditmar Schaub into pieces.

Schaub appeared less than comfortable.

Johannes spoke first, being...personal and not formal, not classist, not stratified, *very modern*, "Ditmar. So, just to be absurdly clear, technically this began before the slaughter at Magdeburg in May of 1631. My family came from Leiden, my grandfather from Scotland. My father had become one of the city's burghers. My mother's side was from...it doesn't matter."

"That's not an explanation, that's a justification. You weren't native to Magdeburg," Schaub said. He crossed his arms. "Not that I don't believe you."

"You're aware, then. We'd lived in Magdeburg for about twelve years." He cleared his throat. "I'm hunting two men in particular. One calls himself by the last name of Grimm, the other is often known by the last name of Chekov."

"Both are...vaguely familiar names. You know, three bombs went off, broke some windows. None of those bombs were huge." Schaub spoke carefully. "That was a distraction, then."

"It certainly was. Likely Grimm's idea," Johannes said, absolutely certain. "Time for them to get away. Do you know that I hoped to God these men would not turn up ever again?"

Johannes could still remember how the blood pooled in the low parts of the streets of Magdeburg, thick as glue. Bodies left where they were cut down, men, women, whole families—unless they were in the way. Then the bodies were dragged and dumped in towering piles, all of them to be left to the carrion birds. *I doubt Tilly burned them unless it was convenient.* Most were eventually scavenged for anything of value before being dumped in the Elbe.

"What are these men to you?"

"Half the reason my Magdeburg died. Spies are spies. Their job it seems was to report weakness, or try to create weakness." Johannes spoke flatly. "It was not politics."

"What was it that I cannot imagine?"

"Carelessness, convincing those in charge of Magdeburg to refuse to negotiate until too late, convinced by things whispered to push that...re-action. Greed. Morality. Opportunity. Ethics. Any and all of the seven deadlies. The city was Protestant, fairly rich, but not as rich as now. These enemies, these monsters, these sons of Cain, passed in and out of the city with impunity for at least a year before the siege, longer even. They smuggled things, even people, into position. They pretended to be what they were not. The more they did, the richer they got."

"You're assuming. It might not be true."

"I believe it to be," he said. "I've read the up-timer accounts. Those are really thin. They didn't live it."

Schaub said, "Your ideas might not be true at all. I think you've been lied to. The fact that they even have any information is a miracle. The *Katholische Liga* had forty thousand men lined up to sack Magdeburg."

"So? They killed everyone I knew." Johannes shrugged. He remembered the moat widening into the river channel, then clinging to the side following out to the river. The stench, the stench! In the shallows floated the bloated bodies of people who had tried to escape. Their bribes must have been disregarded. He had stayed so low in the water scarcely any of him was visible. It helped that the day was dimmed by smoke from the burning city. Only God knew for how long. Time twisted away into a slippery thing, shortening and lengthening at random. It had felt like hours before he came across the boat, but it couldn't have been. The sun had not moved that much.

The boat was a little flat-bottomed oval that was beached just outside the walls. It even had, by some miracle, two paddles. It might have been a fire brigade zille, but seemed too small for that. Its nose was oddly blunted. Without stopping to consider, he swam over and hung onto the little boat's side. He had pushed it along the River Elbe until he thought he might drown from exhaustion—he'd seen enough of that. Some miles upriver, he had rolled into the little boat with the paddles.

Ditmar asked, "Hmmm. Not politics?"

Johannes cleared his throat. He looked towards von Herbert's house down the street. "Simple personal greed. Do you know our good doctor, Herr Lorenz von Herbert? Everyone knows him to a degree. He's CoC for a reason. By the behest of his father and grandfather he was part of the *Katholische Liga*, as were his brothers. He was on the opposite side of the Magdeburg wall to me. Had I known of him then or his brothers, I likely would have killed him, them. Such was my job. Had he or they known of me, the same."

"Assassin, then?" Schaub spoke firmly, maybe a touch warily.

Johannes shrugged. "I did not see it that way. I was a sharpshooter employed by my city Magdeburg to kill the trash or the aristocratic, pick them off on the battlefield, from the city walls. I wasn't the only one." Johannes stopped, coughed, then went on. "Herr von Herbert was doctoring anyone who needed it in the *Katholische Liga*, not fighting but in a medical tent. Although I did see him in action, once."

"All right. In action?" Schaub asked.

"When he is not doctoring he can defend himself very well," Johannes said. It was true, after all.

"Bloody hell! He's deadly? So, what happened?"

Johannes kept staring at the woods behind the house above on the hill, seeing more movement. "He knows I am here in Grantville. We spoke politely about *this issue* some years back. I was given a warning note by that barkeep, Villareal, that something was coming, to stay put so I could speak to von Herbert. He, von Herbert, convinced me to stay here. *"Become a math teacher,"* he said! *"You can guard my children that way. I'll pay you. And you make the teacher's salary."* So, I did. Nothing left to lose. The Thuringen Gardens was having their second *Cinco de Mayo* taco festival about a year after *that* trial and hanging. So, we drank and ate and came to that agreement."

As if he'd not really heard Johannes, Schaub said, "When Villareal's wife was kidnapped and abused?"

Johannes nodded, swallowed. Figuring out how to phrase this was hard. "There's history," he went on. "Herr Lorenz von Herbert's oldest brother, Dietrich, married a French noble lady in a magnificent ceremony in 1613, before the French Court in the king's chapel, when they were at the palace of Fontainebleau. It was by arrangement. No love, initially, I assume. The king, of course, was in attendance. She is, or was, heiress to several estates less than one hundred English miles from the Palatinate border, a couple of castles, a hunting lodge, villages, farms, mills, and the like. The Duchy of Lorraine is relatively nearby, and some small territories belonging to other houses are there too. So that's where Dietrich and Aliénor went, afterwards."

"Still. That doesn't make it not politics."

Johannes shrugged, continued. "Dietrich made the decision to take his family to Rotterdam in late 1630, to the Hague eventually, northeast of it, less than fifteen miles away. He took his family to the New World in May 1631 out of the port at Amsterdam after the slaughter at Magdeburg. Lorenz had sent him a note to get out." He glanced over at Schaub. He coughed a bit. "Dietrich in fact did not participate in the siege. His younger brothers, two of them, were shot, killed. Both shot in the back while in the front line of the *Katholische Liga*. Herr von Herbert thought Dietrich took his family to Tadoussac in Quebec. Those I was connected with thought New Amsterdam, but it might not be either."

Schaub stared at him hard. "You are CoC, then, hardcore?"

"Most definitely CoC. Not hardcore. Service as necessary."

"Before, not mercenary?"

The bitter tone rose. "My father had me, before the unending war, learn assassination, sharpshooting, to benefit our position. I was sick of *that duty* before the slaughter. Old argument, old...guilt. But..." He trailed off into a short, singular cough. His throat hurt from talking so much. He could almost see his past unfold. He stared at the woods across the road.

Johannes had paddled the boat against the current, arms shaking from fatigue, seeing day go and night come twice, the glow of Magdeburg burning lighting up the clouds at night. He'd hidden several times from boats coming down river, pulling up the little boat into the scrubby trees along the Elbe's banks. He had been too tired to cry then, in a numb place beyond horror and terror. Not knowing how many of his family, friends, and companions were dead or alive burned like coal.

Johannes got to just past Glinde. Somehow, he met a fisherman. He'd sold the man that boat for a few coins, a place to sleep, dry clothes, and plain boots and food. He'd lost his weapons in the river. Johannes couldn't remember if that was deliberate on his part. He slept like a dead man for three days. Four days later on May 31, 1631, he started his walk to Rudolstadt. It had been nine days since Magdeburg. He walked maybe one hundred thirty miles at such a slow pace. He did not feel well; he walked sick for three of those weeks. Johannes stopped several times, resting, refueling his energy. Once he stayed put for nearly a week, in a stable with a hayloft, with no one around. His boots needed to be resoled, so he found a punch and a saddle for that, carving up the saddle and making thin leather cords.

He'd arrived in Grantville with a pistol and some ammunition, stolen along the way. He was a different man than he had been, like everyone else who managed to get out.

Six years later, and this was the closest he had gotten to the bastards who, as far as he knew, had made what happened *there* possible.

"All right. Should I believe you?"

"Ask Herr von Herbert who holds the reins on Grimm and Chekhov. Ask him what happened to Grimm under his care when he had to take that leg after it was practically blown off. Ask him why Dietrich disappeared with his wife and children. Ask him who murdered his older brothers, Ludwig and Karl and their wives and children. Ask him about the heir, Erasmus. He wasn't the firstborn but now he's first and the heir and trying to kill any other claimant, with the father's blessing. Ask von Herbert about the poison he was certain Erasmus used to dispose of the grandfather."

Schaub blinked. "Hard to believe." He shook his head.

"Maybe. Erasmus von Herbert is a jealous man; he's what the up-timers call psychotic. I am not certain how that applies. But it is not politics. It is a family feud, a terrible, terrible feud. You will excuse me—I have hunting to do."

"But you're ill?"

"It doesn't matter. This has got to be settled. Besides, you have two young people to speak to. Go inside. I think you will find Maggie—Magdalena Vogel—the more interesting of the pair, but Young Fred is also interesting."

Johannes stalked off. Coughed softly. He missed the thermos of tea.

For a moment, he almost missed Ditmar's comment. The man had replied to his back, "Interviews at this point? Don't be absurd. There's no time."

"Ha! And hell came in the guise of Magdeburg's final *memento mori*—the wrecked wall. Agreed, there's no time."

He walked away. It was so cold, it cut through his cloak and his jacket.

Ditmar Schaub said a few more things. Then, from behind, he bellowed in English, "This is not an academic exercise! Check that residence first!"

Johannes, stopped, turned, threw back in kind. "*Ja*, I know!"

Schaub bellowed again, sarcastically. "No hunting in the dark! You hear me!"

"Ha!" Johannes gazed at the sky and realized the clouds entirely covered the moon in her first quarter.

Surgery, Leahy Medical Center
Nearly 6:00 p.m., February 2, 1637

Amalia noticed the cold. Or rather, her back was cold, which was cause for concern as she heard voices like angels singing. Then something touched her in the arm where she knew she was hurt, and she groaned.

She mumbled and cried. Her eyelids felt so heavy. She managed to moan, "It hurts...", and reached up to her head with her other arm, only to have someone's hand catch hers. The hand squeezed, feeling rather like a skeleton with muscles arranged around the bone. But the hand was warm, then, after a time, felt strong as steel.

"Relax, little one, let me move your arm just a trifle," said a man's deep gravelly voice, soft and gentle. She knew the voice. It was her father.

"Morphine?" Another voice, a woman's, asked. She didn't know her.

"Yes, Barbara, she's due. Has Dr. Adams rescrubbed?" The man's deep voice said.

"He's coming," she said.

The deep gravelly voice said, "I'm glad you're here. Mama, you see how soaked our girl is. Her wounding is nearly battlefield level. You finished donating? Heinrich?"

Heinrich didn't say anything much, just, "No, father. I'm not well enough."

Amalia felt a pang. *I missed him so much.*

"Yes. Just now." Her mother sounded worried. "That tent is cold. How much will be needed, Lorenz?"

Her eyes wouldn't open. Why couldn't she open them? She wanted to see her mother. Her brother.

"A unit or two from each donor, Rosie. As you match her perfectly, the saline drip will make two units possible. I am a type O negative, a universal donor. So they've got a unit from me. They didn't take from Heinrich, but others, including a boy named Gavin, gave the same amount as you. A classmate, I believe."

"There were five of us donating in the tent just now," Rosie said, evenly. "My arm is sore."

Amalia murmured, nearly inaudibly, to anyone, "I want to live."

Dr. Adams' voice was heard. "Good, good. Status, nurse?"

The Barbara-nurse-woman's voice said, "She was being rolled to the morgue, started breathing and yelling, from nothing discernible to awake and alive. We think the bomb blast woke her, dragged her back. Shocked a bunch of people."

"I can imagine," her father's voice said. "Think about it. Hypothermia can sometimes result in hibernation. She did have a pulse...twelve beats per minute. The initial triage missed that." His voice sounded relieved.

Another voice, perhaps Dr. Adams, said, "Well, they're not dead until they are warm and dead. At least that's what the saying was, up-time."

Amalia heard her father say, with realization in his voice, "Hmm, sleep now."

Amalia became aware of lying on her stomach. Something was on her face. Whatever she was breathing was cool and sweet. It was like she was being ignored. There was a prick in her left arm. Things tingled. Someone was cutting her out of her dress, peeling it off, peeling off the blood-soaked shift, washing her in warm water, drying and redressing her. Then everything got quiet.

A door closed. Her father whispered again, "Mama, she lost at least two units of blood, more probably."

It seemed like no time at all passed, but Dr. Adams said in a certain voice, "Not that much. She has a concussion; her ear was ripped half off. Her blood count is down to nine red blood cells per ...well, good might be thirteen or more. We fixed the ear and that, and mended the skin—there and there. Three bullets hit her. Grazed the forehead, hit her in the hip, and got her in the right arm. Missed the vitals. Actually, the femoral artery is bruised, but it'll heal as well."

Her mother asked, "Scars?"

"Some. None to be a horror."

Pediatric Ward, Leahy Medical

When Maggie thought about all of it later, she'd remember her tears and relief.

When she was examined, done, cleaned, the fresh clothes awaited. The woolen shift to mid-thigh, silken cotton trousers, little house slippers, a simple long linen shirt over the shift, and a robe-like jacket in gray that stopped mid-calf. The outfit was warm. She rolled up her hair in a white Turkish towel. No braces for her knees or wrists. She'd have to be careful and manage without those until they got replaced or cleaned.

She was sent to the ward of the least hurt, a pediatric ward. The young orderly escorted her to make sure she got there. The young woman said she was studying to be an LPN. The little pediatric ward had space for four beds. Each bed was just about as narrow as a child's cot, maybe a little bigger than that.

Maggie's orderly said, "Let me make this up for you quickly. It looks hard but the lambswool mattress is on top like so. See, I've fastened it just now, put the canvas cover over it. It's liquid-proof, then the linen sheet. See, this bed is already better. The top sheet now, then the wool blanket, then the duvet—covered. Pillows. See, it's not hard any more. Oh, there is an up-time water toilet and two sinks through that door, over there. I expect you know how to use it. Let me help you into bed. Oh, my word, your hair! Let me help you...there's a comb and a red ribbon. Oh, and a little pot of olive oil." She started on Maggie's hair, drying, detangling, massaging the oil lightly in, combing, plaiting, all very, very fast. "Do you want me to order you supper?"

"Oh, thanks. I'm not hungry."

"All right then, I'll have the kitchen send up herbal tea with honey and a warm bread roll with butter. I'll order breakfast for you. Porridge and walnuts with honey and butter and coffee will arrive around 7:30 a.m. after you've seen the doctor in charge of this ward."

Maggie hesitated. "Okay."

"Good, good. Now rest. Stay in bed if you can. You've had such an awful time today. Oh, oh, Mel Richards has been asking to see you."

Maggie shook her head. "I don't know who that is?"

"Okay. I'll tell her. I'm sure she can wait. She has other things on her plate."

Leahy Medical Center
February 2, 1637

An hour later, Maggie was still wide awake. Tea drunk, fresh warm bread eaten with butter, but she was restless, nervous. *I'm terrified. I should be. What's wrong with me?* Out loud, she said, "I'm going for a walk!"

She did not want to be in her hospital bed, even though it was warm. *I'm not ill. I don't need that sort of care.* There was no one else in the ward, not even a nurse. Her mind fragmented, scattered down its own avenues of fear.

So she walked. The building was shaped more or less like a triangle. Angles. The stairs were too hard to consider. She stood at the bottom of one stairway, looking up. It was clean, warm, and bright. *I'm not going up. My knees would not like it.*

Maggie walked some more, limping, wincing. Her eyes hurt from crying, but it was better than lying in bed.

The dayroom was the first normal thing she'd seen. It faced...what direction? It was dark through the windows, so she couldn't really tell. *This is so confusing.* Its doors were not locked; they opened easily. The tiny brass plaque on the door frame read: *The Arundel Mothers' Dayroom was generously donated by the Earl and Countess of Arundel on May 5, 1636 in honour of their 31st anniversary.* Maggie pushed the door and entered. It was dark outside the windows. She could see the lighting in the other building, towards her left. The two buildings made a small courtyard of sorts.

A white wicker chair, one of several, sat near the tall glass windows. The space was not expansive. There was a stone table next to the chair. A lamp even, with the modern *Edison* bulb lit, casting warm shadows. The other lighting was soft, coming from a handful of wall sconces. *It's as warm as summer here. Might as well stay. Someone will tell me if...* She didn't want to finish that thought. The dayroom had a few potted plants, sweet flowers.

Eventually, an LPN entered. "You gave me a start. You're not in bed," she said.

Maggie turned from looking out the window to looking at the nurse. "I cannot sleep. Is there any word from my friends, Old Fred, Young Fred, Amalia?"

The nurse sighed. "Old Fred is in the level-two triage. Young Fred did say to tell you. As for your friend, Amalia, I cannot speak as I do not know anything yet. Would you like to read a book? Would you like more chamomile tea?"

"You're not going to tell me to go back to bed, are you?"

She shrugged. "What good would that do? I'll have the tea brought here, and I'll send someone with a few books. In the meantime, sit and rest."

Eventually, not long, one of the other LPNs rolled in a cart with the promised chamomile tea and the promised books, all by up-time authors: *Slaughterhouse Five* by Kurt Vonnegut, *And Then There Were None* by Agatha Christie, *Starship Troopers* by Robert Heinlein, *Rite of Passage* by Alexi Panshin. None were terribly appealing, but she did pick up *Rite of Passage*, spending three chapters inside the character Mia's mind. A giant asteroid-based starship and problems! She gave up when she realized that she couldn't really remember what happened in the previous chapter. *I'm worse than I thought.*

There was another book on a table nearby, *Ben Hur* by Lew Wallace. There was a Bible also. She stared at those. Blinked. Tears leaked unnoticed down her cheeks as she gazed into nothing, just the outside for a while. It was snowing harder. Her mind was foggy and strange to her.

In time, quite a while later, there was a knock on the doorframe. Footsteps. A soft voice, a woman's, a nurse's maybe. "We've come to see you, *Fräulein*."

Maggie looked over.

Emergency Room, Leahy Medical Center
Late evening, February 2, 1637

Doctor Adams pulled off his sweat-drenched medical cap. It was almost a full-head sort: down to the ears, finely knitted, and white. The cap had a blessing for divine help for all medical procedures, embroidered in Latin and Hebrew and German along the bottom of the rim. He remembered hearing from somewhere that when the synagogue ladies made some of these, the Christian doctors had asked for the blessing in Latin as well. The caps were a statement. All the nurses and orderlies had the same on their caps. He supposed the synagogue ladies were like a knitting club doing good. He had a good dozen of those caps, just like the rest of the doctors. He was tired. The more he stared at the cap, crumpled in his hands, the tireder he got.

I'll either make it to midnight or sleep on the couch in the staff room again.

He heard a slight cough as Dorothea came in. He appreciated her skills. She was generally pleasant, respectful.

"I have to talk to you." Anxiety filled her voice.

He raised an eyebrow and tried to look alert. "Oh? Surgery?"

"Not exactly." She hesitated, then said, "Jeff."

"Hmmm, I can't think of the last time you used my first name. All right, Dorothea, not surgery. What?"

"Magdeburg. Not surgery, sir."

Jeff felt his hair on the back of his neck rise. He searched her expression, asked, "*Then?*"

She nodded. "*Then.*"

There was awkward silence. Jeff asked, "But not now?"

Dorothea exhaled. "You know we have about three hundred people living here, maybe more, who survived the Magdeburg slaughter? Who all came here for safety?"

Jeff spoke softly. "I didn't know it was that many."

"This matters. No, I'm not from after the siege, I'm...from before the final acts of the siege. We left just a few days before it happened, before the wall was breached. We snuck out and headed south. We got here in late October."

"That isn't a secret. You've been pretty open about it. You were on the road for months?" He leaned forward slightly, arms resting on his knees, staring at her.

She felt jittery. "No. We stopped in safe places. But that's not important."

Doctor Adams studied her face. "You've noticed something, here, today, haven't you?"

Dorothea nodded.

Doctor Adams handled his surgeon's cap, twisted it around, reopened it and did the twist again, responded as Jeff. "You know, this cap is a lot like that kid's toy where you stick your fingers in and pull but have to push in to get loose."

She nodded. "I need to get rid of this memory. I need to tell you. In confidence."

"I'm not a priest."

"I'm not...Christian," she said.

"I figured that out years ago. Not an issue. I have your confidence at heart but if it is something that needs to be said to the police..."

Dorothea nodded, seeming to make up her mind. "I believe I might have seen...two...of the home invaders. I caught a good sight of them two days ago in downtown, near, near, the gunsmithy on Main Street, I don't remember. But that wasn't the first time I'd seen them."

"Why would you think that? Didn't speak?"

She sniffled, blew her nose on a handkerchief. Nodded. "I side-glanced."

"Did they see you?"

"If they did, there was no hint of it. I've seen them before, not here. Jeff, I saw them in Magdeburg in 1631, in March and then again in May, before *we, my family,* ran away. One calls himself Herr Grimm and other names, but Garnerius Toefler is also called Jake, Jacob Chekhov."

"You know them?"

"No. I have *seen* them, though. I saw them downtown several times in the last week, maybe three times together. When I saw them, I recognized them from Magdeburg in March of 1631 and then in early May. I hoped I was wrong."

Jeff, looking her straight in the eyes, asked quietly. "High politics?"

She shook her head. "No. No. No. Spies slipped in and out of Magdeburg for weeks, months before the siege, a long time. We learnt the depths much later."

Jeff leaned forward, rested his elbows on his knees, thought about it, then asked, "Why would you think spies were slipping in and out?

"It makes sense. You know Magdeburg was a Protestant city?"

"Everyone does," he said. "And we all know the stinking high politics—wait, what are you trying to tell me?"

She seemed to hold her breath for a time, weighing options, then said, "My father-in-law brought them home in early March, 1631."

"Hmm."

"Yes he did, Jeff. My father-in-law brought Grimm and his fellow spy to his house in Magdeburg. My husband took umbrage...at his father. We argued, my husband and I, about this. My husband wanted to expose those men, and my father in-law did not want to risk exposure. With all the arguing, well, I wanted our family to leave. It was bad. My husband sent me away to my father's house with our baby, Arabella. He made me pack my clothes and gave me money. He lied to his father, said my mother was ill and needed me. He said he was sending Arabella as she was still a baby. And I was leaving our boys. He—my Shlomo—was supposed to come after, with our boys." She swallowed. "Our boys, Isaac, David, Timotheus, who wasn't even eight yet. They never came. We left without him, any of them. My father and all of our clan slipped out through the gates of Magdeburg just after midnight May seventeenth 1631. Getting through the army lines was insanely difficult, I found out." Dorothea stopped.

Jeff asked, "Were you harmed?"

"No. We were safe, Jeff. It was as if we were invisible. I don't know what to think of that, save the bribes must have been huge."

Jeff Adams looked at his shift's head nurse, again. She was incredibly pale. "All right. I believe you. But the community in Magdeburg..."

Dorothea hesitated, then shook her head. "The *community* was not large, hardly there, maybe a hundred families. Two years ago, I found out that all of my husband's family was dead after the siege but not from the final bits of the siege. When the invaders entered their home..." She sniffled. A single tear escaped. "Everyone, I was told...everyone was already days dead. That my father-in-law was not Jewish after all but had claimed to be from the community in Istanbul. My mother-in-law had also claimed to be from Istanbul but no one from there in that community knew their names. My father paid a lot of money to try to find out. We simply don't know. Proving anything is hard."

Adams just sat there. He looked over Dorothea. She was clearly snow pale. After a time, Adams said, "Magdeburg was stormed and sacked because the defenders kept fighting, declining negotiation."

She shook her head. "No, no, no! The spies lied to everyone. Influenced."

Jeff Adams was quiet for a time, finally speaking after several minutes. "Proofs do not exist. We only have the records we have." He sighed. "There's a game of strategy that makes the game of chess look simple. It is called 'Stones.' This sounds like a piece of a much bigger game."

Dorothea was shaking her head, no, no, no. "Not politics!"

"Dorothea, the defenders kept going even after a breach was made in the city wall. Their actions condemned everyone."

She said, "Surrender was not accepted."

The Day Room, Women and Childrens' Wing, Leahy Medical Center
About 10:30 p.m., February 2, 1637

Dr. Lorenz von Herbert stood just inside the threshold. The wide doorway framed him. He was an intimidating presence: sharp-featured, tall, a mane of dark graying hair. His expression was observant but gave nothing important away. He was careworn, exhausted. He was plainly attired for a *freiherr*. Maggie had the impression he stood between the tick and the tock of time. Next to him was Amalia's mother, Roswitha, Rosie, grim and angry. Amalia's brother, Heinrich, still in his wheelchair, in pain, dressed for ease of transport.

Maggie had never seen them together before. Not forgetting her good manners, she stood and curtsied with difficulty. She straightened, winced, then asked worriedly, "Sir, ma'am, sir, can you tell me anything?"

"Amalia is sleeping," Dr. von Herbert said. "A morphine-induced sleep."

"Oh, oh. She'll pull through, maybe?" Maggie tried to keep her mouth from trembling.

"We are fairly certain of that," Amalia's mother said. "Please call me Rosie."

Amalia's father gave his wife a look, but asked Maggie, "When did our daughter lose consciousness? It's important."

"She was awake when we fled through the cellar door to the garden. There were at least two bodies lying out there. Very bloody. I knew them, your workmen."

"I am so sorry." He paused, in pain. "Go on. I knew them well. It takes betrayal to kill a good sharpshooter."

Maggie swallowed, nodded. "There was a gunshot from behind us. It was so loud, but, but, it did not seem to hit anything. So we kept going. Amalia was crying. I remember Old Fred pulled up in his horse cart, came, picked Amalia up out of my arms, and loaded her in. He climbed back on the cart. Our classmate Young Fred—he's in English and Math with us—helped me into the cart. We raced here. I noticed that Amalia's eyes were opening, shutting, moving under her lids like she was trying not to sleep. The ER sent me to the pediatric ward, but I could not rest, so I came here."

"Thank you." Dr. von Herbert said to his wife, "Amalia was not without vitals too long. It was maybe the corset and where the shot went into her back."

Maggie gasped. A cold feeling swept through her. "You mean?"

The doctor said, "She's only just finished surgery. Dr. Adams attended, I did not. Three bullets. The side of her head, as you know. Her arm right after, which you did not. And her back, which you also did not know of."

A nurse came into the room, whispered to Dr. von Herbert. He nodded.

Rosie glanced at her husband and then son. "Heinrich, please stay with Maggie. She should not be alone."

Heinrich rolled his wheelchair round. "You didn't get wounded, I see."

Maggie looked down at her hands, her crooking fingers. "I already am."

Heinrich very delicately took her hand as if she might break. His eyes were an amazing silvery blue. "I know."

A Week Together

Bjorn Hasseler

*T*his story follows "Reed and Kathy Sue" (Grantville Gazette 64 and IX). Kathy Sue and Reed wrote letters to each other while Reed was deployed in support of Third Division from June 1635 to March 1636. Reed just returned home the previous evening after the events of "The Aftermath" (Grantville Gazette 100). Further on in the new timeline, Kathy Sue will write more letters in "Remember Plymouth" (1637: The Coast of Chaos) and "A Christmas Letter" (A 1632 Christmas).

Grantville
Wednesday, March 19, 1636

"Daddydaddydaddydaddy!"

"Yikes." Three of Reed Burroughs' children clung to him. "I'm sorry, Kathy Sue. I'm leaving you with wound-up kids."

"Pffftt," his wife responded. "Lydia has school. Thomas and Mark just need to run around outside for a while."

"I'll get home as soon as I can. Oh—I don't know what day yet, but can you and the kids come out to Camp Saale?"

Kathy Sue raised an eyebrow. "Family day?"

"They're promoting me."

"Reed! Why didn't you tell me last night? That's wonderful! Congratulations!" Kathy Sue wrapped him up in a hug.

"What's the matter?" Kathy Sue leaned back just a bit to look him in the eyes.

Reed sighed. "Not sure I want it."

She gave him a sympathetic smile. "The paperwork instead of the job?"

"Yeah."

* * *

Reed kissed Kathy Sue at the door, hurried down the front steps, waved, and went off to work. It felt good to think of it that way for a few days, even though he had his rifle slung over one shoulder. Before the Ring of Fire, he'd gone off to Fairmont, where he was the assistant manager of a hardware store. He'd been good at it. A USE Army supply company did the same things: unload truck (or wagon or sleigh), stock, get it to the customer, and run a continuous inventory—with much higher stakes, including the occasional firefight.

He and his men would inspect deliveries, inventory supplies, and make sure everything was ready to issue when Third Division began to arrive. On break, maybe he'd call Kathy Sue to ask if he should pick up anything at the store on the way home—and how much to spend. He kept a small reserve of cash with him, but the USE Army sent most of his pay straight to his and Kathy Sue's joint bank account.

Reed facepalmed right there on the train. *Of course* the officer's commission was a good idea. Kathy Sue wouldn't have to worry quite so much about money. *Crud. I need to apologize tonight.*

Grantville seemed less crowded than when he'd left for Wismar in 1633, but it continued to change. He supposed it was mostly a good thing, but it clashed with his memories of the town he'd grown up in. Maybe they could get the next war over quickly, and he'd be able to come home and get used to it, spend a lot more time with Kathy Sue and the kids.

Reed grabbed a copy of the railroad schedule when he changed trains at Schwarza Junction. He'd have to visit various businesses this week to negotiate for delivery of one thing or another. A USE Army officer would sign the actual contracts. It might even be him. Once they were out of the Golden Corridor, though, they'd have to use imprest a lot more. That worked like petty cash, but on a grand scale.

Camp Saale was smaller than the town of Saalfeld. It contained rows and rows of buildings, the parade field, and a few other facilities. In the winter of 1633-1634, something like nine thousand men had trained here. Now, in 1636, many of the barracks put up that winter were used for other things, including supply. It would be crowded again when Third Division came through.

Someday, I'm going to design a supply base from scratch, Reed told himself. *Not stockpile in infantry barracks with too-small doors or in warehouses limited by how Erfurt is laid out or stashing things here and there and everywhere like we had to do in Wismar.*

* * *

Reed looked their house over as he came home in the early evening. The white with green trim looked decent. A couple spots could use touching up. *Have to find out if we can buy green paint down-time.* The porch was one of the things they'd fixed before moving in, and the repairs seemed to be holding up. There weren't any loose boards, at any rate.

"Sugar, I'm home!" Reed closed the front door, hung his uniform coat in the hall closet, and pulled off his boots.

Kathy Sue popped out of the kitchen at the far end of the hall. She made a beeline for him and threw her arms around his neck.

He gave her a gentle squeeze and a proper kiss. "How are you, Sugar?"

"Just fine. How are you?"

"Pretty good. I got to see quite a bit of Grantville today. It's changed."

Kathy Sue nodded. "Sure has. C'mere."

She raised a finger to her lips, then took his hand and led him into the kitchen.

Lydia stood on a chair, examining bottles from the spice rack on the wall and putting them back. Mary was in the playpen over in one corner.

Lydia turned around. "Hi, Daddy! I'm organizing the spice rack!"

"I see. How are you deciding what goes where?"

"Oh, I started alphabetically. But then I decided the ones that smell nice should be easy to reach. The bottom row smells nice, the middle row smells okay, and the top row I can barely reach smells yucky."

Kathy Sue gave him an amused look. "The boys, not to be outdone, are upstairs organizing their toys according to how big a boom they make."

Reed grinned. "I know adult men who use the same method."

"Daddydaddy! Come see!"

Reed inspected his daughter's work. "Very nice, honey. I see you're stocked up on mint."

Six-year-old Lydia nodded enthusiastically. "It's my favorite."

"Lot of horseradish, too."

"Yuck," Lydia pronounced.

"That's from my mom," Kathy told him. "She said Dad isn't the only one who can make weapons-grade stuff. She sells it to the grocery stores."

Reed laughed. Then he unscrewed the lid and sniffed. "Wow! She's not kidding about weapons-grade."

He peered at the other bottles on the spice rack. "It's a pretty good selection."

"Yeah. Grow, chop, and grind your own."

"Looks like you're doing fine," Reed told her.

"I just follow directions from both our moms and try not to kill the plants in the windowsills and in the sunroom."

"How did you decide what to grow?"

Kathy Sue smiled. "The part about following directions from both our moms? The Grange and the master gardeners portion it out. A certain amount goes back into seed. More seed if we're short of a spice, less if we've got a surplus."

"What system do they use to keep track?"

His wife grinned. "Association by story and genealogy and scandal."

Reed laughed. "I can just see the little old ladies.... Seriously, though, does anybody write this down?"

"Maybe? I think it's more along the lines of 'Mary Sue and her people must have thirty basil plants between them.'"

"That sounds suspiciously like 'Hans and the guys can probably make fifty barrels.' And then there aren't fifty barrels." Reed gave a wry smile. "The world is not divided into up-timers and down-timers. It's divided into organizers and TLARs."

"What's a tee-lar?" his wife asked.

"That Looks About Right."

Kathy Sue giggled.

"Mommy? Can I dump these two together?" Lydia asked.

Kathy Sue's reply was wary. "What are they?"

"Orange-e-o and garlic."

"No!" Kathy Sue and Reed exclaimed together.

Lydia turned, a puzzled expression on her face. "Why not? They both smell yucky."

Her parents exchanged glances.

"They're different flavors," Kathy Sue explained. "And they're not yucky when mixed with something. You like spaghetti, right?"

Lydia's "yeah" was pretty much a German "*ja*."

"I use a little of each in the sauce."

"You do?" Lydia sounded downright betrayed.

"You even like oregano chicken," Kathy Sue told her. "If I cut it up..." she whispered to Reed.

"Tasty chicken cubes!" the girl recalled.

"Oregano is part of the tasty."

"Are you sure, Mommy?"

"Yes, I'm sure."

"Oh, all right."

Reed pursed his lips to keep from laughing and saw Kathy Sue doing the same. Then she asked, "Do you hear the boys?"

"Nooooo." Reed headed for the stairs.

Halfway up, he heard a crash and yelp. Someone burst into tears. Reed charged into the boys' room and almost turned an ankle on a building block.

Mark was in full cry, and Thomas was trying to comfort him.

"Uh-oh. What happened, Mark?"

The boy continued to cry. Reed picked him up and held him.

"Daddy, he pulled out the bottom block and the whole tower fell on him," Thomas said.

"It fell on purpose!" Mark wailed.

"Yeah, gravity's like that," Reed murmured.

"Bad grav'y!"

* * *

Kathy Sue gratefully sank into the sofa cushions and did nothing for a few minutes. She'd just decided to sit up, real soon now, when Reed entered the living room.

"Hey, Sugar."

Kathy Sue sat up and slid over. Reed eased himself down beside her.

"They're all in bed," Reed reported. "At least for now."

"Mary will wake up to nurse," Kathy Sue told him. "I'm glad the kids wanted Daddy to tuck them in."

Reed frowned. "They'll want me to stay."

"I know, Reed. We'll deal with it. The girls kicked me out of the kitchen. They're cleaning up. We usually end up in here. Talk, watch a TV show."

"Is that a hint to stay or to clear out?" Reed asked.

"Let's let them have the living room tonight." Kathy Sue made the suggestion with a smile.

Reed stood, bent at the knees, and scooped up his wife.

Kathy Sue put her arms around his neck. "This is all *An Officer and a Gentleman*," she murmured.

"Funny you should mention that."

Reed carried her into the hallway and headed up the stairs. Kathy Sue didn't ask about his comment. She didn't want to distract him on the stairs, although he carried her easily.

At the top of the stairs, Reed turned right, toward the back of the house. They passed the girls' room on the left and a bathroom on the right. Kathy reached out and opened the door to the master bedroom before Reed turned sideways to fit them through. The addition a previous owner had made to the back of the house wasn't quite as high or as wide as the rest of the house, but since the new bedroom had its own bathroom, it had become the master bedroom.

Reed started to set Kathy Sue down on the bed, but she put a hand on his chest.

"Bounce?" She asked it the same way the kids would.

Reed obligingly dropped her on the mattress. Kathy Sue giggled.

"Shh, you'll wake the kids." Reed's delivery was deadpan.

"Then they'll be in here wanting to bounce on the bed. But funny I should mention what?"

"*An Officer and a Gentleman.*" Reed sat down next to her with a sigh. "Sugar, the promotion is more pay, and I'm sorry I forgot that part."

Kathy Sue made a noise of dismissal. "You wanted to teach the men, and I've heard Dad say a professional army relies on NCOs and logistics a couple hundred times. I think he told James when he was five, so I would have been seven or eight."

Her face clouded over for a moment.

"James and Chris and Kim." Reed named her brother and his brother and sister, all of whom had been living in Fairmont when the Ring of Fire happened.

"I hope they're okay," Kathy Sue whispered. "I hope James finally asked Kim out. They lost almost everybody. Maybe they got married." She managed a wan smile. "More Burroughs-Alcom kids."

"What would they be, to ours?" her husband asked.

"You could ask my mom. She'll know for sure."

"Oh, no, Sugar. *You* ask. I don't want to have to explain I haven't interviewed every German I've met to ask if they know any Fritzes or Meinderts."

Kathy Sue giggled.

"But I really am sorry about not accepting a promotion earlier. It would have been more money." Reed named a sum.

"Per month? Reed, I still would have taken out the mortgage and put it into OPM. Maybe bought something extra every couple months. But it wouldn't be worth you not liking what you're doing."

Reed kissed her.

Once they came up for air, Kathy Sue asked the question. "Are you okay with being an officer?"

"Yeah. It'll be less time physically moving and inventorying supplies but more time training officers."

"Want to practice on the kids tomorrow?"

Kathy Sue asked whimsically, but Reed caught the current underneath.

"Training them to put stuff where it belongs?"

"Yeah. I can manage to get them to contain the mess for Sunday, but the rest of the time..."

"Um..."

Kathy Sue smiled. "I bet I know what you're going to say. 'It's not that bad, Sugar. I've seen supply depots way messier than this.'"

Reed laughed. "Yup. That is what I was going to say. And I have." He looked down at his wife, who was still lying on their bed. "How does it bother you?"

"I don't like stepping over stuff, especially in the hall and on the stairs. The rest...as long as it's not actually in the way or getting broken...I just don't want it to look a mess, y'know?"

"I remember." Reed smiled. "When we moved in, you gave the moving boxes dirty looks until they went away."

"I did not!" Another giggle spoiled Kathy Sue's indignation. "You were just as bad." Then she pulled Reed down next to her.

"Probably. Face it, Sugar. Both our families have the quartermaster gene."

"We civilians call it being a control freak," Kathy Sue murmured.

Reed smiled. "As long as we're making the kids clean up because we want it that way instead of other people wanting it."

"Well, Anna Maria, Rosina, and Magdalena. They live here, too. If our moms or aunts walked in, they'd start picking things up."

"Yeah," Reed agreed. "They don't mean anything by it, but...the quartermaster gene, y'know. I've learned to let guys run their own supply depot."

"Really?" Kathy Sue looked over from where she lay. "I thought you'd want all the widgets in rows over here, and all the doohickeys stacked up over there."

Reed laughed. "I do. But if they've got a system that works, I'd just make them mad. Of course, if they can't supply what they're supposed to, on schedule—and find it all—I've got a new system for them."

Kathy Sue smirked. "So, tomorrow night do you want to give the kids a system?"

"Sure. Let them know they're helping you, throw in a little enlightened self-interest..."

"They do like the clear space. Me, too. It's nice when everything in the living room is back on the shelves so we have room for the next activity."

"I'll see what I can do."

"Thanks."

"Y'know, it might be more comfortable under the covers," Reed pointed out.

"Good point." Kathy Sue sat up. "But I needed that."

Her husband's eyebrows went up. "A rest before bed? How close to the edge are you, Kathy Sue?"

"Probably closer than I should be but no closer than everybody else." She smiled. "I might not have gotten as much as sleep as normal last night."

"Me, neither. We should probably go to sleep right away."

"Don't you dare." Kathy Sue rolled over on her side so she could kiss Reed.

Mary began to cry.

Kathy Sue pulled back. "Timing." She rolled to her feet and retrieved their youngest, speaking to her quietly. "You need to cut out the late-night snacks, yes, you do."

Mary's only response was a grasping motion.

"I know you want milk."

Kathy Sue settled herself back on the bed, leaning against the headboard and unbuttoning her blouse. "Sorry for killing the mood," she told Reed.

Reed waved it away.

Kathy Sue looked down at their daughter. "The whole mommy milk thing is going away soon. You'll get all-bottle. Yes you will." She sighed. "And now we see who can stay awake longer."

"Anything I can do?" Reed asked.

Kathy Sue sent a smile his way. "Backrub?"

Reed towed her to the middle of the double bed and settled in behind her. He kneaded her shoulders.

"Oh, that feels good," she murmured. After a few moments, she added, "I've missed this."

"Me, too."

"Mary will be a while. What you want to talk about?"

"Tell me about the church."

"I think it's going well. Several of the ladies are really growing. Usually a bunch of kids take over our kids' rooms for Sunday school. The *Bibelgesellschaft* girls and their friends are filling in the high school and college & careers age groups. But you know the verse in the greetings in 1 Corinthians 16. 'For a wide door for effective service has opened to me, and there are many adversaries.' I feel like that sometimes. The adversaries usually aren't other people—or at least not people trying to be adversaries. It's stuff like getting hung up on each other's denominations or the kids needing to clean their rooms Saturday night or something going wrong with the scheduled preacher."

"I told my guys services will be here this Sunday." Reed paused momentarily as Kathy Sue's blouse suddenly went taut. "What is having a few dads around going to do?"

"I think it'll be nice. Whole families can go to church together. Are there likely to be some single guys?"

"Some." Since Reed was behind Kathy Sue, he didn't even try not to smile.

"Bunch of single girls, too. Lots of distractions."

"Yeah, I remember this cute girl inviting me to church," Reed said.

"Just pointing out there may have been a sermon or two we didn't really pay attention to." Kathy Sue looked down. "Ready to change sides, Mary? You have to let go of the blouse. You're all tangled up. Come on, let go."

Mary began to fuss. Kathy Sue finally convinced her to let go. She set Mary in her lap and reached both arms behind her.

"Help, please? I think this is in everyone's way."

Reed obligingly helped Kathy Sue out of her top.

"Speaking of distractions..." He resumed the backrub.

"Oh, right. I scheduled a potluck after the service Sunday. Your folks want us to come over for dinner tomorrow night. They're inviting the whole clan. Whoever's in Grantville, at least. Then my folks want us to come over Friday night. Mom and Dad are coming down from Erfurt." Kathy Sue reached back with one hand, caught Reed's wrist, and gave it a quick squeeze. "I'm sorry. I know you don't want to be out late."

"Yeah, but I'd be in worse trouble if I didn't show up at both sets of parents. Your plan, Sugar?"

"I just offered a suggestion and let our moms run with it." Kathy Sue couldn't have sounded more demure.

"Uh-huh. My dad's whole family?"

"If Melanie is there, they'll play nice."

"That doesn't make any sense. Oh, it's true," Reed assured his wife. "It just doesn't make sense, seeing how my grandparents split up over Melanie."

"No guarantees from Mel or Press," Kathy Sue warned. "They'll try, but Maria and Thomas will be there, and nobody will say anything in front of them."

"Also true," Reed agreed. "I do want to see them, since they're my brother and sister now. How is law enforcement in Grantville? Besides busy."

"Press and Mel can give you a full report. If they can't make it, Astrid Schäubin from NESS will be here Sunday."

"What's NESS?"

"Neustatter's European Security Service. They started guarding the *Bibelgesellschaft* a couple years ago. Georg Meisner and Barbara Kellarmännin are both in the *Bibelgesellschaft*, but they do some work for Press, too.

"NESS's core group had already left Pastor Holz's independent Lutheran church. Last spring, after the riots and Fred Jordan falling off the roof over in Ohrdruf, Georg asked NESS to ask Holz to ease up on his demonstrations. They read one of his sermons, and Otto asked the *Bibelgesellschaft* girls why pastors like Holz preach about the law so much. Marta Engelsbergin gave him the verse in Romans 10 about Christ being the end of the law. So they went to the Anabaptist and Baptist services to ask Joe Jenkins and Brother Green. Georg asked Astrid out, and she's been going to the Baptist church since then. Barbara and Otto started dating not long after."

"Huh."

"There's this group of library researchers—the good kind. A Dutch girl, Josyntjie, has come once or twice. She's dating Astrid's cousin. Eva Želivský from the *Unitas Fratrum* is dating Astrid's brother. One of the others is a monk from Bohemia. I haven't met him. Pri...Pray..."

"Praemonstratensian?" Reed asked.

"Yes!" Kathy looked over her shoulder. "Why do you know tha—? Wait a minute! You said there's a monk you couldn't write about. Are our monk and your monk buddies?"

"Pretty sure," Reed answered. "White robe?"

"Yeah. Huh."

"Great intel briefing. Thanks, Sugar."

"Pffft. I'm not an agent. I'm just a wife and mom."

"You are a wife and mom, Kathy Sue, but there's no 'just' about it. And you're basically running a house church."

"I am *not* a pastor."

"Nope. From your letters and how you've explained things, I can tell you're the team mom. Again, no 'just' about it. In the first century, they'd probably call you a deaconess."

"I refuse to be some stern old lady."

"Of course. You'd rather help. You organize, and unless I miss my guess, listen and provide guidance and teaching."

"I think they teach me more than I teach them. I just, you know, facilitate."

"Uh-huh. I think the Bible word for that is 'serve.' You're doing an awesome job."

"Aw, thanks."

"I know because the *Unitas Fratrum* in Prague got your Bible studies. A couple of 'em made their way down to us in České Budějovice."

"The Bible studies or the *Unitas Fratrum*?"

"Both. A couple of them came down with one of the supply shipments and brought copies they got from their wives. Careful! If you keep turning around in surprise, you're going to get a crick in your neck."

"You're not wrong." Kathy Sue touched her neck. Reed kneaded gently, and Kathy Sue sighed.

"Thanks. Oh, that feels so good."

"We were going to make copies ourselves, but Mike—General Stearns—ordered us to move out. You have originals, right?"

"Yeah. Speaking of which, how is your sermon coming along?"

"Same as usual. Read the Bible, pray, and think it over when I can. It's Mark 10:35-45. Mostly the last verse, 'For even the Son of Man did not come to be served, but to serve, and to give His life a ransom for many.' It hasn't gelled yet."

"We've got a few minutes to pray before Mary passes out."

* * *

"Please give Reed the words to preach each week and keep him safe."

"Thank you for keeping Kathy Sue, Lydia, Thomas, Mark, and Mary safe and healthy. Please watch over them always. In the name of the Father and of the Son and of the Holy Spirit."

"Amen."

After a moment, Reed whispered, "Is Mary asleep?"

"A few minutes ago," Kathy Sue whispered back. "I'll go tuck her in."

She was back in a couple minutes and settled onto the bed behind Reed. "Your turn for a backrub."

A couple minutes passed. Reed murmured, "Oh, that feels great."

"Wanna unbutton that?"

Reed peeled off his shirt.

"I think you should take me with you." Kathy Sue's tone was whimsical. She put her arms around Reed's neck from behind. "You must have something I can stow away in."

"That's a very fun and terrifying idea," Reed told her.

Her words were a bit sad. "I know."

"We should take a trip," Reed said. "When the war's over. Just us."

"That sounds fun. Where to?" Kathy Sue's fingers kneaded just below his shoulder blades.

"Mm. We could see what Magdeburg is like."

"Sounds good. We could go to Wismar, too, and see how they're doing."

"Train or boat?" Reed asked.

"Mm. Tough one. They both sound romantic."

"Not much privacy, though."

"What about a cabin on a lake?" Kathy Sue asked.

Reed turned his head to the right. "Is this a real place?"

Kathy Sue leaned forward on the same side, and her long hair fell over her husband's shoulder. "The count and countess of Rudolstadt bought a place in the eastern lobe of West Virginia County and built a dam. So there's a lake now. It's just a few miles from Camp Saale. Normal camp stuff, but also arts and sciences lectures and demonstrations. People got the idea from some place up-time with a long name I don't remember."

Reed was intrigued. "How's this work? Is it regular-people camp? Or for the *adel*?"

"It's supposed to be everyone, mingling. I only know about it because a bunch of Anabaptists are on staff. They're having their own camp meeting there at the end of June, and then they'll run the place for everyone else in July and August."

"We should definitely look into that." Reed really meant it, but he was very aware his beautiful wife, who until yesterday he hadn't seen in nine months, was partially undressed and draped all over him.

Thursday, March 20, 1636

Warm blankets were great. Hot water was great. Time with Kathy Sue was the best. Now Reed had to go to work on something like three or four hours of sleep. He had no idea how Kathy Sue managed to make breakfast, keep three kids occupied, and a fourth on track to catch the bus while talking with Anna Maria, Rosina, and Magdalena.

He gave Kathy Sue a hug from behind. "How are you awake and chipper, Sugar?"

She turned her head for a kiss, holding kitchen implements clear. "Oh, this is a sprint. Mark and Mary and I are good until nine or ten, and then we all crash for a nap. Thomas can play quietly."

"You are incredible."

Kathy Sue gave him her best smile.

"Breakfast is almost ready. We've got eggs, actual bacon, and almost-cereal. Mush, to be honest. Porridge, if you're reading Goldilocks."

"Real bacon?"

"Yup. Do you know what they'll have you do today?"

"We're getting some new guys. I'm not sure of the details yet, but I'll teach them Supply."

"'Stack it, track it, sign for it'?"

Reed smiled. "Maybe I *should* hide you in a duffel bag."

"Maybe you should." Kathy Sue smiled back. "You'll still be able to do some of the hands-on work, right?"

"I intend to make a point of it," Reed stated.

"Good. I know it's a good example and all that." Kathy Sue lowered her voice. "Speaking of strong, you've been personally moving a lot of supplies, the way you carried me upstairs last night. I think it's a good idea if you keep working alongside your men."

Reed grinned. "So noted."

"Do you want to come home this afternoon and then drive over? Or meet us there?"

"Is there a right answer? Either works."

Kathy Sue shrugged. "Not really. We wouldn't want to get there too long ahead of you versus getting four kids out the door almost as soon as you get home. It's just which one you want to deal with."

"I'll come home first. But can you drive? Thanks, Sugar."

They kissed. Reed hugged the kids goodbye and left for Camp Saale.

* * *

Captain Steiner called Reed into his borrowed office. Another officer, also wearing a captain's double bar insignia, waited. Reed vaguely recalled him—from one of Third Division's camps, no doubt.

"At ease, Sergeant Burroughs."

Reed stood at ease without relaxing one bit. He was fairly sure he wasn't in trouble— which meant *dat Gute-Idee-Fee* had struck. The Good Idea Fairy was trouble, up-time or down-time.

"Reed, I think you have finished training me and the XO"—he pronounced it "iks oh"—"so you will become the XO of a new supply company—as an *erster leutnant*."

Reed blinked. "*First* lieutenant, sir?"

"We are not making you a second lieutenant. We need you to train second lieutenants."

He handed Reed half a dozen stitched-cloth insignia. The narrow black straps had a thin outline of silver thread, and a single bar of silver thread at each end.

Reed kept his expression impassive. This was both good and bad. Good, because as the executive officer, he'd oversee training. Bad, because he'd have to train the captain, too. Young officers usually wanted a command in one of the combat arms. The other captain in the room looked young.

"This is *Hauptmann* Johannes Stauttenbecker. *Hauptmann* Stauttenbecker, about-to-be *Erster Leutnant* Reed Burroughs."

Reed saluted. Stauttenbecker returned it crisply—a good sign—and then shook hands.

"How old are you, *Wachtmeister* Burroughs?"

"Thirty-one, sir."

"*Exzellent!* I am twenty-four myself, and everyone will feel more comfortable with a mature XO." He pronounced it "iks oh" as well and smiled, although the expression seemed brittle to Reed. "Wilhelm Tieben and I have both been promoted, but there was only one *hauptmann*'s slot open in the Witige Regiment. *Hauptmann* Tieben now has an infantry company...and I have orders to organize the Fifty-First Supply Company."

Reed kept his mouth shut. He had definite opinions, some of which he'd come to on his own as an assistant manager at the hardware store. Others he'd picked up from his father-in-law, and some he'd reached by watching Mike Stearns. They boiled down to: Tieben would promote faster, but Stauttenbecker would promote further—assuming he was level-headed about the whole thing.

"*Oberst* Hachmester already explained it to me," Stauttenbecker continued. "So I will tell you honestly I am half-convinced. But I won't do anything stupid, like taking a supply company into battle if there is any choice at all."

Reed relaxed a little. "You sound more than half-convinced, then, sir."

"Your company will get some experienced sergeants, too," Captain Steiner told Stauttenbecker. "Sergeant Burroughs, leave me a few."

"Yes, sir. Who is the next *wachtmeister*, sir?"

"What is your recommendation, Sergeant?"

The supply companies were smaller than infantry companies. The *wachtmeister* was the first sergeant, and two *feldwebel* were platoon sergeants. Each led a squad and usually had a second squad led by a sergeant working with them, for a total of sixty rank-and-file.

Reed's answer was instant. "Sergeant James Dunn, sir."

"*Und* which sergeants are you taking?"

Two supply companies would not remain together for long, just until the Fifty-First Supply got up to speed. Then both would be in the rotation, bringing supplies to the front, delivering them, and going back for another load.

Arguably, it made more sense to keep particular supply companies with the division and use the rest to bring the supplies forward, but it wasn't how the USE Army worked. One company might be retained at the front for a while, but they cycled. Everyone got experience with procurement, transport, and distribution. Plus, the constant rotation of personnel was supposed to cut down on anyone's ability to make corrupt deals or systematically pilfer items.

The small congregation Reed pastored was about to get divided.

Start with the partnerships.

"Do you expect Second Supply to stay paired up with the same MP company, sir? Or will it divide to cover both the Second and the Fifty-First?"

"They're staying with us, Reed. The Fifty-First is getting a new MP company that's been training at Jena."

"Charles McDow is the MP company's *wachtmeister*, and he works well with Sergeant Hans Moschel. I recommend promoting Moschel to *feldwebel*, sir."

"May I assume you want Bruce Reynolds and Alexander Ebenhöch, then?"

"Yes, sir. Reynolds is senior to Moschel, so he should be *wachtmeister* for the Fifty-First. I'd like Ebenhöch for one of the Fifty-First's *feldwebel*. That gives each company one sergeant promoted to *feldwebel*."

"We will have to promote a pair of corporals two ranks to *feldwebel*," Captain Steiner pointed out. "Which two do you recommend?"

"Caspar Treiber for the Second, and Friedrich Patzscheldt for the Fifty-First," Reed answered. "Simply because Treiber is used to working with Dunn and Patzscheldt is used to working with me. No sense making it any harder than it already is."

"Agreed."

Once they'd divided up the corporals and privates by the simple expedient of keeping squads with their sergeants, Captain Stauttenbecker and Sergeant Burroughs took their leave.

Reed breathed a sigh of relief. They'd make the right decisions militarily. He could still try to be a good spiritual influence on Bruce Reynolds. Charlie McDow was a fairly serious Presbyterian, and Hans and Caspar were both very Lutheran. Jimmy Dunn was Disciples of Christ, married to a Baptist. Reed figured they'd manage something.

"I read the sergeants' files," Stauttenbecker said. "I saw little to differentiate between them. Are you satisfied with the division of men?"

"Yes, sir."

"Two up-timers in each company. In ours, the XO and the *wachtmeister*."

Reed knew what he hadn't asked.

"Sergeant Reynolds is a *feldwebel*, and Sergeant Ebenhöch is a sergeant. If we did it the other way around, Ebenhöch gets promoted twice, and Reynolds not at all. Besides, Reynolds needs a challenge, and Ebenhöch has a tendency to take too much on himself. In this case, going by seniority is also what's best for the company and the two of them."

"*Und* this is why I let you pick," Stauttenbecker told him. "That is not in either man's file. I did see you four up-timers—you, Reynolds, Dunn, and McDow—have served together off and on since the Ring of Fire. How long have you known them?"

"Bruce is a year older than me, and Jimmy is a year younger. We went to school together. I don't remember ever not knowing them, although we weren't in the same group of friends. Charlie is ten or twelve years older than the three of us. I knew him well enough to say hello, but I can't say we ever had more than a casual conversation before the Ring of Fire."

"One thing concerns me, Sergeant Burroughs—in *your* file. It says you conduct church services, but not what kind."

"Non-denominational Christian."

Captain Stauttenbecker's shook himself. "That is not...you cannot *do* that."

"Yes, sir, I can."

"The *oberst* of any regiment could object."

"One could, sir. A few officers did object to one of my sermons in Poland. Colonel Straley explained freedom of religion to them."

"Colonel Straley?"

"He commands the volley gun regiment. He's with General Torstensson's army. At least, he was last I heard, sir."

Captain Stauttenbecker looked stubborn. "*Wachtmeister* Burroughs, provost marshals and even government officials may object to your preaching."

Reed kept his words and tone respectful. "I am happy to talk with them. We can go see General Stearns together."

Captain Stauttenbecker *still* looked stubborn, but he changed the subject.

"The new men should be here tomorrow. What do you plan to teach them first?"

"When do we leave, sir?"

"Wednesday morning."

"Let's start with an inspection. *Hauptmann* Stauttenbecker, I do not care if they *pass* the inspection or not. What I want to learn is whether they've been properly equipped themselves."

"I am sure they will be sent down from Magdeburg with uniforms, weapons, and canteens."

"Yes, sir, I expect so. What I am looking for is *telogreikas*—the padded winter coats—extra socks, the condition of their boots. Winter is not over yet, and they have to be able to function in it before they can supply anyone else. Then we will have mud season before true spring. Here's what I'd like to do...."

After Reed explained what up-time veterans called *layout*, Stauttenbecker said, "Do it." Then he asked, "Are you married?"

"Yes, sir."

"I am not. Not yet. I have noticed the commander's wife is usually in charge of communicating with the soldiers' families, seeing if they need anything."

"Yes, sir."

Reed tried to figure out how to avoid dumping it on Kathy Sue.

* * *

"Reed!" Joella Burroughs ran out of the house and threw her arms around Reed as soon as he got out of the minivan.

"Hi, Mom. Missed you."

"Oh, I missed you, too, Reed. How are you? Come in, come in."

"Gramma! Gramma!" The kids swarmed out of the car and ran to hug Grandma Burroughs.

"We'll be right in," Reed promised. He turned to help Kathy Sue. She took Mary and the diaper bag, while Reed slung the other kids' bag over one shoulder and carried the vegetables.

Inside, Mark Burroughs gave them time to set everything down before shaking hands. "How are you doing, son?"

"Doing okay, Dad," Reed answered. "We were making good progress getting everyone resupplied outside Dresden when our company got called away to help a Swedish unit. Can't say as I mind, since it meant we got sent on to Grantville for a few days."

"A Swedish unit? Got anything to do with those cavalrymen who rode in ten days back?"

"If it was the *Västgöta*," Reed answered. "Did everything go okay?"

Mark Burroughs shrugged. "They had some sort of ceremony with Liz Carstairs, Scott Blackwell, and Vic Saluzzo. So, I guess so."

"Glad to hear it," Reed said. "Good guys, just ended up under Banér."

"Grampa! Grampa! Grampa!"

Mark Burroughs got pulled away by his grandchildren.

"Not everyone is going to make it tonight," Joella told them. "Freeman and Janet are on their way. David and Cindy and their kids are coming, but Austin and Kimberly and their kids are in Magdeburg, and Anissa and Travis and their kids are in Nuremberg. Stella can't make it, and the Pilchers are out of town, too. Mel said she's pretty sure she and Press and the kids will eventually get here, though. Your Grampa Johnson isn't well enough to come, but Gramma Johnson should be here shortly. Maria and Thomas are in the living room."

"Thanks, Mom," Reed said. One aunt and uncle were expected, along with one of his cousins and his family. Another aunt and uncle would be there with their kids. So would the two German teenagers his parents had adopted. And his grandmother, of course.

"C'mon, kids, let's say hi." Reed led them into the other room.

Lydia immediately ran to Maria Ziegler for a hug.

Tommy stared at Thomas Ziegler curiously. "You're not old enough to be our uncle," he stated.

Thomas laughed. "I'm not really your uncle."

"Sure you are," Reed said. "How's eighth grade?"

Thomas made a face. "Hard. Maria got to drop out."

"When she turned eighteen," Reed reminded him. "After tenth grade. You've got four years left, so may as well finish."

He felt much more strongly about it, but it was up to Thomas and their parents, not him.

"I want to join the Army," Thomas continued. "Do you have time to help me learn to shoot better?"

"Sorry, Thomas," Reed told him. "I'm at Camp Saale for just a few days, and then we're moving out. I don't think I can fit it in this time. You can ask Kathy Sue, though."

Thomas looked a little dubious.

Reed chalked that up to normal teenage skepticism. "Kathy Sue and I and our dads used to go on deer hunting dates."

Thomas burst out laughing.

Good.

During dinner, Reed answered everyone's questions as best he could.

"A lot of what I do is like when someone would pull into the hardware store in the middle of winter and buy enough to fill his truck. Find the exact items and load everything while trying not to freeze."

"Oh, we have warm clothing, gloves, and socks. We had warm barracks in České Budějovice, and we've been fine through the winter. After we got to Dresden, though, and were out in the field day after day, I got pretty cold by the time I came in for the night."

"It's not so much I can't say as nobody's told me. You can probably figure it out, though."

He managed to parry with, "Is there anything I need to know about what's happening in Grantville?"

That set off a flurry of conversation. In short order, Reed learned the details of the split at First Baptist Church, the perceived need for more schools, and quite a bit about local politics.

Not everyone in his extended family was in agreement on the school bond issue. He kept up just long enough to find out it would not involve redistricting and then lost track of the minutiae.

* * *

Kathy Sue returned from tucking in Mary.

"Seeing everyone was fun," Reed said.

"It was." Kathy Sue smiled and picked the opposite side of the bed tonight.

Reed slid under the covers next to her. "Something came up today, Kathy Sue."

"What's that?"

"I met my new captain. He is uncomfortable with me preaching."

Kathy Sue frowned, and Reed continued on.

"Captain Stauttenbecker is twenty-four and single. He asked if you would take charge of family support and communication."

"Me?"

Reed sighed. "I know you're burning the candle at both ends, Kathy Sue. I should have told him no right away, but—"

Kathy Sue's hand on his arm stopped him. "I can't do it by myself. But maybe the church can."

"That's a fascinating idea."

"Nobody has to join the church or anything like that. We'll just adopt the company."

"That'll make heads explode," Reed predicted.

"The down-timers won't even blink," Kathy Sue countered. "At least not until I tell them it's our new mission field."

Reed grinned. "Some have families here, some in Magdeburg. The single guys are from all over."

"Oh! So, letters. Reed, that's just like mailing Bible studies around and asking for prayer requests, just said differently."

"Advocating for soldiers and families can be a ton of work."

Kathy Sue grinned. "Nah, I'll just facilitate. Do the team mom thing. Invite them to church. If we help each other, it'll be easier. The ceremony is Saturday, right? I can talk to them then. Oh! Do you need a new uniform?"

"Just new insignia on the old ones."

"I'll do it tomorrow. Simpler than letter jackets, really."

Reed shook his head. "You're amazing."

"Aww. It's so nice you believe that."

"Sugar, I think we're both really tired."

"I know." She sighed. "Pray, cuddle, and pass out?"

They made it through a few verses in Ephesians.

Reed prayed. "Father, thank you for making us and sending Jesus to save us. Help us remember Your greatness and love. Please show us what to do about the company's families."

Kathy Sue took over. "Lord Jesus, thank you for dying for us and rising again. Please give us rest and strength."

"Holy Spirit, please help us remember how great and loving You are as we go about our lives tomorrow. Amen." Reed put the Bible on the end table next to the bed and turned off the light.

Kathy Sue lay back against her pillow and rolled onto her side. Reed scooted down in the bed and pulled the covers up over both of them. Kathy Sue's top arm slid around his waist. He put his around her back, higher up. Then he leaned in and kissed her.

"How are you doing, really?" Kathy Sue asked. "You got really quiet a couple times at your parents'."

"Some things people were talking about are hard to relate to right now. Those things don't matter to me now."

"You're...not on edge, exactly, but alert. All the time."

"Yeah. The Army had somebody talk to us. Hypervigilance, they called it. Helps us stay alive in the field, and we can't just shut it off all at once at home. Once the wars are over and I'm home, it'll fade."

"Like the dreams?"

"Yeah. How 'bout you, Sugar?"

"I can't remember dreaming for a while now."

Reed frowned. "Kathy Sue? No bad dreams is nice and all, but maybe take all the kids to Tommy's daycare once in a while? Take the day off, sleep, do whatever you want."

"That sounds...wonderful."

"Any chance I can take my wife on a date?"

Kathy Sue's eyes snapped open. "Keep talking."

"Monday night, want to cash in on your mom's 'we'd love to have the kids over sometime.' Sugar, you should do this every so often. I bet a lot of people would give you a nice time to yourself."

"Oh, I couldn't!" Kathie Sue exclaimed. "I don't want to impose. Everyone works so hard."

"Sugar, I wish I were here."

"Me, too, but don't start. You're where you need to be."

Kathy Sue is probably right. "So, about our date..."

"What kind of date do you want?" Kathy Sue asked.

"You mean like hunting in camo vs shakes at the mall? How 'bout something normal?"

Even in the dark, Kathy Sue looked interested. "Go on."

"Dinner and a movie?"

"Do you mean on the TV or at the theater?"

"Theater? For-real movies?"

"Yeah." Kathy Sue looked a little surprised.

"Huh. Cool. I didn't know we have movies. I wonder what else I've missed?"

"Oh, Reed." Kathy Sue's voice broke. It sounded like that one had really gotten to her.

"Hey, hey. Never mind." Reed took her hand. "Where do you want to eat? I'm not sure I'm up-to-date on the options."

"Lots of new options," Kathy Sue told him. "Freedom Arches, although our booth is gone, and they don't have milkshakes."

She sounded sad, so Reed shook his head.

"The Gardens, of course. Tyler's, if you want fancy. McDougal's. Castalanni Brothers and Marcantonio's."

"Would pizza undercut the idea of a nice date?"

"Not at all! Pizza's fine. And somebody reinvented root beer."

Reed sighed. "That sounds wonderful."

"It really does," Kathy Sue agreed.

Friday, March 21, 1636

Reed went off to Camp Saale, Lydia caught the bus, and Kathy Sue put Mary in the playpen in a corner of the kitchen while she started the pot roast for dinner at her parents'. Then, she read the kids a couple stories before she got Mary down for a nap. Mark took longer to settle, and Tommy was wired.

"We went to Grampa and Gramma's on yesterday night, and we're going to *other* Grampa and Gramma's tonight!" the four-and-a-half-year-old kept repeating.

"Yes, Tommy. Can you play quietly while Mark and Mary and I take a nap?"

"Can I play loud?"

"No, you'll wake us up."

At some point, Kathy Sue dozed on the sofa. She awoke with a start and a sense it was too quiet. Tommy, however, was building something with both blocks and toy boxes. She dropped back onto the couch.

Mark woke up first and needed attention. Kathy Sue got started on the laundry afterwards.

"Thank you, Father God, that the washer and dryer still work," she whispered. "Please keep them running."

Eventually she'd probably end up with down-time-made appliances, but so far the washer, dryer, stove, refrigerator, freezer, and furnace were all hanging in there. They'd had a scare with the furnace but it had been fixable...that time.

Thinking about the kitchen appliances reminded Kathy Sue it was nearly time for lunch. She also needed to add vegetables to the pot roast. She'd heard about a new way to do this. It sounded like a water-based crock pot made of down-time materials coupled with a meat thermometer. But she knew her trusty up-time crock pots, and a family gathering wasn't the time to experiment. Not that anyone would say anything. Her mom would have everything else just right, and Kathy Sue wanted to measure up.

She smiled in remembrance. Once she got her driver's license, she'd also gotten a part-time job at the Christian bookstore over in Fairmont. A lot of the books had been Bible studies and devotionals, but the store had a Christian fiction section, and she'd learned a little about what made a good book and what didn't.

Kathy Sue had encountered a coincidence she found hilarious. Her mother's name was Mary Sue. It fit. Just not in the usual negative way. Mary Sue Fritz Alcom was really good at, well, everything: sewing and other needlecrafts, cooking, gardening, raising a family... *Being a good influence on Dad.*

It made being her daughter a little challenging. Kathy Sue couldn't even share the humor. Grantville had never been a hotbed of literary analysis, and jokes weren't funny if you had to explain them.

So, Mom asking her to bring pot roast was...fraught. Pot roast wasn't hard to make, but Kathy Sue wanted it to be *perfect*—and having Mary Sue for a mom meant she'd learned to cook pretty darn well. Her mom was trusting her with the main dish, but at the same time, one that a mother with little children could handle. It wasn't like she'd asked Kathy Sue to mix, knead, and bake bread. Mary Sue never bought bread at the store, of course, except for when Kathy Sue and her brother James had begged for it as a treat.

Sometimes even we happy people have issues. She finished chunking the carrots and tossed them in, followed by the onions and potatoes. She stirred with a wooden spoon, added a different combination of herbs and spices to each, and put the lids back on. It started to smell good.

Some up-time lunch standbys were gone. Peanut butter was not regular-ly available, at least not in Kathy Sue's price range. Bologna was, but Mark wouldn't eat it, and Mary wasn't interested yet. Mark *would* eat thinly sliced salami—go figure—so Kathy Sue put it under a layer of cheese and made cheese toast for Tommy, Mark, and herself. She left off the salami for Mary. She also warmed up some leftover soup and cut up more carrots, this time into carrot sticks. Finally, she poured milk into sippy cups for the boys.

The kids dawdled with lunch, and then the boys ran off to play while she nursed Mary. Mary promptly passed out, and Kathy Sue put her in the playpen with a light blanket. She could hear the boys creating a mess in the living room. She retrieved her Bible and notes from the bookshelf there and sat down at the kitchen table.

The women's Bible study had started Luke at the beginning of the year, and this Sunday afternoon they'd discuss Jesus healing the paralyzed man in chapter five. Kathy Sue wrote down questions in pen, dipping it in an inkwell as necessary. She indented each so she could go back to number them in pencil once she thought she had a plan for the study.

Then she went to the hallway closet and found Reed's second uniform coat. The lieutenant's straps were in the inside pocket, along with a folded cheat sheet. It *was* a lot like sewing the interlocking GHS on a letter jacket, only this time she was carefully ripping stitches to take the *wachtmeister*'s rank insignia off each sleeve. Three chevrons and two rockers, now replaced with a silver bar on a shoulder strap. Those were easy enough, especially with the cheat sheet for guidance.

By the time the school bus dropped Lydia off, the boys were tired. Kathy Sue turned the television on. Children's programming was limited, but the station ran a half-hour program a couple times a day and followed the afternoon one with an up-time VHS recording, often *Sesame Street* or *Mister Rogers*. It gave the kids a chance to learn something while they recharged.

Before Reed arrived home, Anna Maria, Rosina, and Magdalena were in and out, having Friday night plans with a group of friends.

* * *

"Reed! Welcome! So glad to see you!" Mary Sue Alcom exclaimed.

"Glad to be here," he replied. "Thanks for having us over. Where would you like this?"

"Right over there on the counter. Don't thank us. The Rieses were kind enough to host us all."

"Is your house," Margaretha Ries stated. "*Und* we learn whenever you are here."

Kathy Sue grinned. Her father and Reed had been stationed in Wismar in the winter of 1633-1634. When she, her mother, Lydia, Tommy, and Mark had been able to join them in the summer of 1634, her mother had rented the house to the Rieses, with a clause that if the Alcoms could stay in the house when they were in Grantville, she'd teach them everything she could about up-time cooking and sewing.

Margaretha and her two daughters wore dresses cut in a down-time style, but in the bright colors of Stone dyes, with rickrack trim straight out of the 1970s. It worked surprisingly well. *Inspired by Mary Sue*, Kathy Sue thought to herself. And she knew Margaretha could do amazing things with vegetables. *Hope the pot roasts measure up.*

"Now, Reed, you and Garland forget about the wars for a few minutes, all right?" Mary Sue darted a look at her husband before plugging in Kathy Sue's crock pots.

"Yes, ma'am," Reed answered.

Garland gave them a lopsided grin. "I got here about five minutes ahead of you. Had to check on someone. Got nothing to do with these wars."

"Sure it don't," his father-in-law Byron Fritz said. "Then why'd you make me wait in the car?"

Kathy Sue had noted a faint emphasis on *these*, and filed it away for some other time.

"How've you been, Reed?" Garland asked.

"Oh, I think tired covers it." Reed grinned. "But this week's great. Get up, go to work, come home, spend time with Kathy Sue and the kids."

"Daddy is here for a week," Lydia contributed.

"Then he moves Army stuff!" Tommy added.

"Yep," Garland agreed. "Amateurs study tactics. Professionals study logistics."

Mary Sue grinned and shook a wooden spoon at her husband.

"What's 'gistics?" Tommy asked.

Soon the fifteen of them were seated around the dining room table and a card table set up for the older kids. Garland prayed, and plates were filled with pot roast, vegetables, and bread and passed down the table.

When seconds were dished up, Garland paused between bites long enough to say, "This one's different."

"First one had Italian seasoning," Kathy Sue told him. "This one is more West Virginia. Y'know, Season All and stuff."

Her dad took another bite. "Yep, sure is." His eyes narrowed. "Honey, how do you have Season All?"

"I don't. I did what Mom did and wrote down the ingredients on the bottle before I cut the label off and turned it in at the library."

Garland Alcom snorted. "So you're telling me somewhere in that collection of tech trees in the library, there's one of spices drawn on a big swath of the local paper, detailing how we can make Season All?"

"Those charts helped us lick a whole bunch of problems with spinning and weaving," Byron told him.

"It's not complicated, dear," Mary Sue told Garland. "Unlike your stuff, there aren't any precursors. We just have to grow the plants, grind them, and mix to taste."

"I know you asked us not to bring up Army stuff," Reed said, "but would you happen to have any connection to the flavor packets we're starting to see?"

"Flavor packets? Like those little bitty things in up-time MREs?" Garland asked.

"Yeah, pretty much. Somebody's reinvented ramen. Or almost reinvented it. These packets show up with it."

Mary Sue smiled. "It's possible some of my basil found its way to you, then."

"I think maybe some of your mint, too." Reed shook his head. "I wouldn't have thought to flavor ramen with mint, but the troops I've talked with like it better than any of the other flavors except juniper berries. Of course, their preferred solution is to cook the ramen in any sort of meat juice rather than water, and their *really* preferred solution is to eat something else entirely."

"Makes sense," Garland said. "How's the church doing?"

"Well, I think," Reed said. "Allowing for I really should have gone to Bible college, but then Kathy Sue and I would have missed the Ring of Fire..."

"So stipulated," his father-in-law acknowledged. "We're here; they're not. Do what we can."

Reed nodded, but it was Kathy Sue who spoke up.

"The *Bibelgesellschaft* can get us some of the information you would have gotten in Bible college or seminary, Reed. Joe and Marta Engelsberg are doing what they can—they're brother and sister—and so is Al Green.

But he's now pastor of Mountain Top Baptist and starting a seminary up there."

"Sounds like that might be the only game in town."

Kathy Sue shook her head. "Kat doesn't think so—Katharina Meisnerin. She's going with Joe Engelsberg. Joe is likely going to be an Anabaptist pastor, so he feels he needs to put in at least a year at Mountain Top. If Kat goes, she'll end up in the wives group. The best place to develop her gifts is university. She and Marta Engelsberg want to go to U of Prague."

Reed blinked. "Prague?"

"U of Jena won't let them in the theology program."

Reed nodded slowly. "Prague might. The *Unitas Fratrum* are still working on how much they can afford to trust Wallenstein. They've been cautiously testing the limits, and Comenius is in charge of the university."

"So, young men," Mary Sue summarized. "But what about young women?"

"Well, the *Unitas Fratrum* does have the usual down-time limits on what women can do," Reed answered, "and in some ways the information you sent on them becoming Moravians reinforces that. Separate groups of women, with the older ones in charge. The biggest thing the girls have going for them, though, Sugar, is *you*."

"Me?"

"Yep, you. Remember, the *Unitas Fratrum* has copies of your Bible studies. I think they might see Katharina and Marta as under your authority."

"They know way more than I do," Kathy Sue protested.

"That may be," Mary Sue put in, "but you're catching up fast. I've heard it in what you've said and written over the last few months. You've got more experience, and I get the impression you're their big sister."

"I get frowny faces if I use high-falutin' words like 'deaconess.'" Reed failed to suppress his grin.

"Don't make me sound old." Kathy Sue's stern protest was spoiled by an escaping giggle. "The girls are smart—and driven. Intense."

Garland grinned. "On a mission..."

"Well, yeah, probably. Kat and Marta want to go to university. Alicia and Nona want to be missionaries to North America."

"Alicia and Nona?" her father asked.

"Alicia Rice and Nona Dobbs."

"You're related to Alicia, Reed." Mary Sue dropped that into the conversation. "So are you, Kathy Sue. Just give me a minute. The charts are in the bottom of the china cabinet."

Kathy Sue exchanged amused looks with Reed while her mother opened the bottom doors of the hardwood cabinet and shifted a couple stacks of dishes to reach several large pieces of cardstock in back.

Mary Sue passed her husband a bowl of vegetables to clear some space on the table. "Margaretha, these are just wonderful." Her finger traced back over generations. "See, Loyal Johnson, your Grandma Johnson's ancestor."

Reed nodded politely. Kathy Sue saw a wariness in his eyes, though. Wondering how much Mary Sue knew about Grandma Johnson's kids, probably.

"Now I saw Loyal Johnson in the Rice's genealogy, too. I don't remember exactly where, because I was more interested in the Baxters and the Thwaite sisters. I don't think the genealogy club ever figured out everything they wanted to know about them." Mary Sue pulled another chart from the stack and placed it on top. "See, here are Jim Baxter and Bessie Thwaite again. My great-grandparents."

Kathy Sue asked a question a bit quickly. "How closely are we each related to Alicia?"

"Third, fourth, fifth cousins. Something like that. Closer to you, Kathy Sue, than to you, Reed."

"I see." Reed grinned a bit ruefully. "I suppose before the Ring of Fire I was probably around a lot of third, fourth, and fifth cousins every day and didn't know it."

"That's probably true in a lot of small towns," Mary Sue agreed. "Speaking of such things..."

Kathy Sue saw the wary look was still in her husband's eyes, but he was more relaxed, on safe ground here.

"Have you found any Meinderts or Fritzes in your travels?"

Saturday, March 22, 1636

Kathy Sue pulled up to the gate at Camp Saale and rolled down her window.

"Serg—Lieutenant Burroughs and family."

The MP made eye contact with Reed and waved them through. Kathy Sue found the parking lot.

Reed came around and opened her door, then they opened the van doors for the kids, who were in their Sunday best.

"Stay clean," Kathy Sue told them. "Don't play in the mud."

Reed walked Kathy Sue and the kids to the edge of the parade field. "They don't have a reviewing stand. Saving wood and metal for something more important is a good grasp of priorities, but the families might have to spread out along the edge of the field to see what's going on."

"Not a problem."

A while later, it was on the verge of becoming a problem as their kids joined other kids running around.

Despite the dress she wore, Kathy Sue caught Lydia and Tommy. "Slow down. Just walk. We don't want mud or grass stains on your nice clothes."

"Can we play walk-tag?" came Lydia's eager request. "Sometimes we play it at recess. You can't run."

"As long as you're just walking." Kathy Sue was dubious about how long it would remain walk-tag, but the kids held it together until both sets of grandparents arrived. Soon after, they all heard someone calling cadence.

Moms and grandparents gathered their children as men in ranks entered the field. They marched to the edge of the field, stopping in two blocks.

"*Hauptmann* Stauttenbecker, front and center!"

One of the men who'd been off to the side came forward, made a squared-off turn, stopped, and saluted. Someone returned the salute. Kathy Sue heard the formal assumption of command phrases.

"First Sergeant Reed Burroughs, front and center!"

"Daddy!" Mark exclaimed.

Reed stepped up next to Stauttenbecker.

"*Wachtmeister* Burroughs, you are hereby promoted to first lieutenant and assigned as executive officer of the Fifty-First Supply Company." More formal phrases followed.

Kathy Sue recognized her cue and handed Mary off to her mom. She joined Reed at the front of the formation. USE soldiers' ranks were stitched on their coats, whether chevrons on the sleeve for non-commissioned officers or officer's insignia on the front-to-back shoulder straps reminiscent of up-time American Civil War uniforms. It meant the easiest way to "pin on" a newly promoted soldier's insignia was to prepare a uniform ahead of time and change coats. Laundresses often doubled as unit seamstresses, but, if practical, a soldier's wife or betrothed sewed on the rank insignia and buttoned the coat for the first time.

Reed removed his coat, and Kathy Sue presented the one draped over her arm. She helped Reed put it on and buttoned the uniform coat.

Kathy Sue kissed his cheek. "Praying for you. Stay safe," she murmured.

As Kathy Sue returned to the edge of the field, she heard, "*Feldwebel* Charles McDow, *Feldwebel* Bruce Reynolds, front and center!"

Kathy Sue watched the rest of the promotions and clapped in the appropriate places.

After the last promotion was made, the new captain put the men at ease and approached Kathy Sue.

"Frau Burroughs, *Ich heisse Hauptmann* Johannes Stauttenbecker."

"*Guten Tag, Herr Hauptmann.*"

"*Erster Leutnant* Burroughs told me that your church is adopting the company. To be the, ah, network, for families."

"Yes, sir."

"If I let him continue preaching?"

"*Nein.* You should do that anyway. We are adopting your company anyway."

Stauttenbecker stood there a moment, obviously weighing the options. "Done and done. *Danke,* Frau Burroughs."

"You're welcome."

Stauttenbecker retrieved the microphone from another officer. "Lunch will be served outside the barracks. Families, please see Frau Burroughs with any concerns you have."

Kathy Sue approached the officer with the microphone. "May I borrow that, please?

"May I have your attention? We will join our men for lunch in a few minutes. If you need anything while the men are in the field, we're here for each other. Don't leave without giving me your names and contact information, and I'll give you mine."

While those who were interested got to see the barracks, Kathy Sue made a quick scan and saw each grandparent had one of her kids. She smiled her thanks and rummaged in the diaper bag for her clipboard. She'd seen the notebook Astrid Schäubin carried and bought the full-size version. The front and back covers were thin boards, and two curved wooden half-circles jutted out of the top front like horns, curling back and ending in wooden knobs. Those unscrewed so she could add or remove individual pages from the two-ring notebook. Then she fished out one of the toy wooden barrels the coopery sold. The lid fastened tightly, and the inside was just big enough to hold an inkwell. Her quill fit in an old pencil case.

"You are prepared," one of the other wives observed.

Kathy Sue smiled as she slid a writing sleeve over her right forearm. "I have to write things down or I'll forget them. Mommy brain."

Over the next few minutes, Kathy Sue learned a lot. She was taking notes when Reed slid onto the picnic table bench beside her.

"Names, addresses, a couple phone numbers, and one email address—and some things to look into."

"Excellent. We can cross-reference it with my table of organization." Reed kept his eyes moving as he spoke. "Lunch is just about ready."

He stood. "I'll say grace, and y'all can get in the lunch line. After that, *Hauptmann* Stauttenbecker is giving you the rest of the day off. Tomorrow, church services here at Camp Saale are Catholic at 9, Calvinist at 10, and Lutheran at 11. There are churches in Saalfeld and Grantville. Many of them have information posted on the bulletin boards. You're welcome to join Kathy Sue and me for church at our house at 10 and Bible study at 2."

Reed prayed, and everyone got in line.

"Kathy Sue! I had no idea you were running the family group!" came her mother's voice.

"It goes with Reed's promotion. But it's really the church adopting the company."

Mary Sue Alcom sat down next to her daughter. Mary, whom she was carrying, immediately reached for her mother.

"Aww." Kathy Sue capped the ink and dropped the inkwell back into the toy barrel first. "C'mere."

"Do you need a hand? I've been in a few of these groups over the years." Mary Sue looked around. "I like this better than the mandatory fun days up-time."

"I'm hoping it's mostly listening to what people need and finding out who can help."

"Pretty much. It'll be a fair few trips out here to Camp Saale. I can watch the kids for you."

"Thanks, Mom."

* * *

The Burroughses arrived home late in the afternoon. The three oldest kids immediately ran upstairs to change into play clothes. As did Reed and Kathy Sue. She threw a load in the washing machine, and they sat down with Reed's files.

Once they'd matched everyone up, Kathy Sue asked, "Do you want to make burgers for dinner?"

"Definitely. No burgers at the company picnic definitely messed with my head." Reed looked around. "Where are Anna Maria, Rosina, and Magdalena?"

"Dorothea is hosting the singles tonight," Kathy Sue told him.

"A safe dating environment with enough chaperones to satisfy reasonable people?"

"Exactly. We have it here, oh, every couple months or so. But it's not something I can go help with when it's somewhere else. I've learned facilitating doesn't mean being part of everything."

Reed gave her a squeeze. "Are you okay with that?"

Kathy Sue hugged him back. "I'm fine, Reed. I'll work on getting out a bit more. But especially during the winter, there's a lot to be said for tucking the kids in and having a cup of non-tea tea. C'mon, let's make burgers so we can tuck them in at a reasonable hour."

Lydia came into the kitchen. "I'm hungry."

"We're about to make dinner. Do you want to help?"

"Okay."

"How are we stocked on fixings?" Reed asked.

Kathy Sue rummaged through the refrigerator. "We've got kale instead of lettuce, and the cheese is different than up-time. I think the ketchup is pretty close, but it's getting harder to remember. Mustard, onions, and pickles. Fries are a lot of work, so I usually make hunting camp potatoes."

"We have those in the Army," Reed told Lydia. "Someone named them *jäger* fries, which down-timers think is strange, because most of them didn't eat potatoes before the Ring of Fire."

"No fries?" Lydia asked.

"Nope, but we'll use some of the spices you organized. Want to shake them in?"

"*Ja!*"

* * *

Once the kids were in bed, Reed finished up tomorrow's sermon.

"Oh!"

Kathy Sue looked up from across the kitchen table where she was working on the next Bible study from Luke. "What?"

"'For even the Son of Man came not to be served, but to serve, and to give His life as a ransom for many.' Except I looked up 'serve' in Strong's Concordance, and this verse isn't there. Strong's is King James Version."

"And you're reading New American Standard Bible."

"Yeah, this gets me every so often." Reed grimaced. "I guess I'd better pack that KJV your parents got me way back when. It's more weight, and it's so seventeenth-century."

Kathy Sue giggled. "I'll go get it."

She returned a couple minutes later.

"Thanks, Sugar."

Reed quickly found the verse. "'For even the Son of Man came not to be ministered unto, but to minister, and to give his life a ransom for many.'" He flipped pages in Strong's. "Yep, here it is. Minister."

"This feels like a translation difference," Kathy Sue said.

Reed looked surprised. "Right?"

"As opposed to a Greek variant," she clarified. "We could call the Brethren settlement just to be sure."

"Seriously?"

Kathy Sue nodded. "I usually just wait for the next Sunday and ask the *Bibelgesellschaft* girls. Especially Kat."

"I wish I could pick up some Greek," Reed said.

"Me, too. That I could learn it, I mean. Both of us, really." Kathy Sue sat there a moment. "I mail Bible studies. What if we mailed the Greek book, one lesson at a time?"

"That sounds great, Sugar, but I don't know if I could keep up, especially with officer paperwork."

"There's no deadline. I'll send a few, and you can say in your letters if it's too fast or too slow. With the supply company families, I probably can't go very fast, either. Maybe we can muddle through it together?"

"Long-distance together?" Reed smiled.

"I'm sure Kat would be happy to answer questions. Joe Engelsberg, too, so guys teach guys. Besides, it'll give Kat and Joe something to do together."

"Are you matchmaking?"

"No! I never liked when people did that to us. But I can see, and Kat and Joe have finally upgraded from good buddies to courting. Just in time for her to go off to college."

"Well, if they can help us with Greek, we can probably offer a few suggestions on long-distance relationships. Which reminds me...do we want to make any changes to our letters?"

"Just speed up the mail. I don't have any changes. Do you?"

"Nope," Reed said. "Like you said, faster mail, more time to write, come home sooner."

Sunday, March 23, 1636

"All the sectors are clean, Daddy! We can move the furniture!"

Tommy disappeared out of the kitchen as quickly as he had burst in.

Despite wearing his suit and a tie for the first time in years, Reed grabbed one end of the coffee table. Soon it was in the dining room, and the dining room chairs were in the living room.

The doorbell rang. Two girls entered, both dressed in up-time blouses and skirts, bearing baskets of rolls and a couple of pies. They looked almost alike.

Kathy Sue handled introductions. "Girls, this is Reed. Reed, you remember Alicia Rice. And this is Amalia Ramsenthalerin."

They exchanged greetings, then Reed said, "My mom says we're third cousins or so. I thought for a moment you were sisters, and I could not remember you at all, Amalia."

"We get that a lot," Alicia told him. "Nursery and children's church upstairs as usual?"

"Yes, please," Kathy Sue answered.

"Nona has special permission to be here today, but I brought the tape recorder anyway," Alicia said. "We'll listen to the sermon later and pass it around."

Dorothea and Elisabetha arrived with their husbands and children, closely followed by a whole group of Brethren. Men from Reed's unit arrived, some with their families. A few of the wives were already regulars. Anna Maria directed everyone with food to the kitchen, where Rosina organized things. Magdalena got all the kids upstairs.

Kathy Sue kept up a whispered commentary. "NESS, and more of them than I expected. Astrid Schäubin and Regina Drehmann in the lead, the rest of the Drehmanns, Eva Želivský and Hjalmar Schaub, Otto Brenner..."

A tall broad-shouldered man stopped and extended a hand. "Edgar Neustatter."

"Reed Burroughs."

They shook.

"I've been wanting to meet you," Neustatter said. "Heard about you when someone handed me a clipboard after Alte Veste and told me to sign my name. Also heard you might've had something to do with a troop of *Västgöta* who rode by the office."

Reed laughed. "Yes and yes. I understand you guard the *Bibelgesellschaft*."

"And try not to cause too much trouble."

"You can believe as much of that as you want, Reed," Press Richards called.

"Good to meet you, Neustatter. Press, Mel, glad you could make it."

Chief Richards glanced into the living room. "I realize it's a special occasion, but if it gets this big often, you need to get with Chief Matheny, Kathy Sue."

A couple minutes later, as Reed stepped over people to get to the far end of the living room, he decided Press had a point. Kathy Sue started out right behind him, but he lost track of her immediately. He should not be able to lose his wife in their own living room—it just wasn't that big.

Then he saw first one, then another, person had stopped Kathy Sue for a greeting, request, or piece of information. It shouldn't have been a surprise, he realized. She could dodge the word deaconess all she wanted—he couldn't disagree that it conjured images of a spinster great-aunt—but it was what was going on here. Reed intended to watch the Fifty-First Supply Company carefully for the same dynamic. When he found them, he'd promote those facilitators to corporal.

Kathy Sue reached the front, and, as they'd worked out, she greeted everyone in Amideutsch.

"Welcome to a house church in Grantville! I realize it's crowded, and this is at least twice as many people as usual. In case you're wondering why a house church when you can step outside and see five church buildings just within the bend of Buffalo Creek that sets off the historic district, we are a multidenominational congregation. Alphabetically, Anabaptist, Arminian, Baptist, Calvinist, Celtic, Lutheran, Methodist, nondenominational, and Roman Catholic. If I missed you, call it out or let me know afterwards. Usually, we rotate preachers from what I've come to think of as the big five denominations, but my husband's unit is here for a few days, so Reed's going to preach."

Reed picked up from there in the same language. "I've been preaching wherever I'm stationed, usually for a few men in my unit and some others. We were in Bohemia up until a month ago, and a few *Unitas Fratrum*

Hussites worshiped with us. In some cases, wives and children have been worshiping here while their husbands and fathers are in the field with me. It's nice to be together."

Kathy Sue took over. "We know some of you are visiting today. Thank you very much for coming. You are welcome back anytime. Some of our regulars worship elsewhere and then come here, or come here only when it's their denomination's turn to preach. That is fine with us. Follow where the Lord leads, and it might not be here. But today, stay for lunch. There's plenty for all of you."

She found a place to sit on the floor, and Reed opened the service.

"We gather in the name of the Father and of the Son and of the Holy Spirit." Some crossed themselves; most didn't. Reed wasn't a big fan of liturgy, but most down-timers were, and even the Anabaptists tended to be okay with something simple and doctrinal.

"Lord Jesus, we worship You. We confess we have sinned and fall short of what You intend for us. Please fill us with Your Holy Spirit and help us do better. Thank You for everyone You have put around us and for everything You have provided for us. Please keep us safe from sickness, accident, and war. Show us how we can serve You and each other. Amen."

One of the down-time ladies began singing. Others joined in. Reed recognized the praise song from the 1980s. It was *a capella* out of a lack of musicians rather than any particular conviction.

Other songs followed, and then Reed opened a time of prayer. *People pray for the same things up-time and down-time,* he reflected. *Just the details are different.*

Then Reed stood up. The top of the television set made a reasonable platform for his Bible and notes.

"Garland, would you pray for the sermon, please?"

Kathy Sue's father was wedged in a corner and didn't bother trying to stand.

"Father God, we ask you to give Reed the words you want said this morning. Help him speak the truth and keep him from error. Amen."

"Thank you. Please open your Bibles to Mark chapter ten, starting at verse thirty-five." He gave them some time to find it before he began reading.

"'...and to give his life as a ransom for many.'"

Reed paused a moment. "This sermon is one of the ones where I'm talking to myself first, and y'all can listen in. I think you'll find it applies to you, too.

"In this passage..."

Sometime later, Reed concluded, "'...shall be your servant.' One of you Greek students, what word is this?"

"*Diakonos*!" one of the girls called out.

"Thanks. This is the word we get the English word deacon from. Leaders are supposed to be servants. And if you think about the whole New Testament, how many places are there where we're supposed to submit to each other? That word is *hupotasso*, and it's a military term. It means to get in rank under someone's command. It doesn't mean you're better or worse, just that person's in charge. So we should think of everyone else as outranking us. At the same time, they're thinking that way toward us, so don't take advantage of them. It's like a giant web of helping and loving each other.

"We know we each have a long way to go, and we won't get all the way there until the Lord glorifies us. But you're doing good. Keep it up and depend on God to help. Let's pray."

* * *

"Good sermon, Reed." Press shook his hand.

"Thanks."

"And you didn't holler at us even once."

"I'm sure there are places to improve, but part of the congregation is here and part of it's deployed. So best to let the Holy Spirit nudge people if He thinks they need it."

A couple others made similar comments. Reed also received several "so happy to finally meet you" greetings. A few people left, but most stayed for lunch.

Soon many of the men drifted outside to where Garland had his propane grill set up.

Reed passed through the kitchen. "I'm going to run upstairs and change into something more suited to grilling," he told Kathy Sue. "Is there anything you need me to do?"

"Nope. Here. It's chicory not-coffee. It's still late winter out there."

"Thanks."

Kathy Sue turned to the high schoolers. "Girls, would you help Alicia and Amalia bring the kids downstairs? We'll put them around the dining room table."

She was somewhat surprised to see Nona's brother Blaine helping. Then Kathy Sue remembered what she'd said to Reed about single girls and smiled to herself. *Looks like Reed's troops have competition.*

The regulars took charge of setting out lunch. Soon a line stretched from the kitchen down the hall to the front door.

Once people were eating, Reed found Kathy Sue in the kitchen. "Your Bible study is at two, isn't it?"

"Yeah, but..."

Reed shook his head. "No, it's important. Go ahead with it. We guys will watch the kids."

Kathy Sue gave him a quick squeeze. "I know what you're doing."

* * *

"We made lots of friends," Tommy announced. "Hans and Freddy and Gerd and..."

Reed reached for a pencil. "Can you tell me about them?"

"Hans is four. He lives in Sa...sa..."

"Saalfeld?"

"*Ja*! *Und* Freddy has a long name and two sisters. He's five. And..."

Lydia interrupted. "One of his sisters is Maria. She's tall."

Reed took notes.

"What are you up to, Reed?" Kathy Sue asked.

"I'm planning to match the kids to their parents and make us each a copy."

"Ah, got it. Kids, don't forget to eat."

Tommy set his jaw. "I don't like soup."

"You liked soup last week."

"Not anymore."

"You need more than milk and crackers."

"I want goo!" Mark proclaimed.

Reed raised an eyebrow.

"Goulash." Kathy Sue explained. "That takes time to make."

"Tomorrow?"

"Tomorrow is Monday, and you're going to Grandma and Grandpa Burroughs."

"Yay!"

After eventually getting some soup into the boys, Reed and Kathy Sue started to clean up.

Magdalena playfully shook a finger at them. "Go. We will take care of this."

Reed looked dubious.

"Go," Magdalena repeated.

They went. The kids wanted to play a game, and Lydia explained the rules.

"You set up your dominoes and take turns rolling the marbles at everyone else's. Whoever has the last dominoes standing wins."

"They made this up," Kathy Sue whispered. "Sometimes there are points."

Amidst falling dominoes, enthusiastic shouts, and the occasional protest, Kathy Sue nudged Reed and nodded toward where Mark had fallen asleep on the carpet.

"Two down. We should go upstairs."

"Mo-om!"

"Lydia and Tommy, you should find your bags and pick out clothes for Tuesday."

"Are we staying overnight at Gramma and Grampa's?"

"Yes."

"Come on, Tommy!"

Kathy Sue smiled as they thundered up the stairs. "I'll clean up sector five myself, and then we can get everyone tucked in."

Monday, March 24, 1636

"How dressy is this?" Reed called from the bedroom.

Kathy Sue came out of the bathroom wearing a dark green velour sweater and a long black skirt. Her brown hair spilled over her shoulders.

Reed whistled. "I'll find a tie."

Castalanni Brothers was crowded. They ordered a medium sausage and pepperoni pizza and drinks. By the time the pizza came, Reed had claimed a round high-top table.

"Are you okay standing?"

"That's why I wore boots instead of heels," Kathy Sue answered. "Well, and it's March."

Reed handed Kathy Sue a slice on a plate, then took one for himself.

"Lord, thank you there's enough food and that we get some of our up-time favorites."

"Amen."

"This is really good," Reed declared a couple minutes later.

"Mm-hmm," Kathy Sue agreed. "I should come by and pick up a pizza for dinner once a while."

"Anything you want to talk about?"

Kathy Sue gave him a sad smile. "Do you mean before Wednesday?"

Reed grimaced. "Yeah."

"Well, we should definitely write letters again."

"Oh, yeah. Send your Bible studies. We'll pass 'em out."

Kathy Sue's expression turned mischievous. "Send your sermons, Reed."

Reed grimaced. "I don't know if I can. Minute a page, right? If I talk for twenty minutes..."

"Not word for word," Kathy Sue said. "Just your notes. How Pastor Townsend in Fairmont showed you how to do it."

"Okay. Dunno if they'll be clear, but I sure won't have time to write out twenty pages."

"Right. People will figure it out if they put their minds to it. Besides, learning Greek would be a better use of your time."

Reed smiled as he served them each another slice of pizza. "I like how you think I'll just casually learn Greek."

Kathy returned the grin. "Oh, I'm telling myself if all the high schoolers can do it, so can we. Plus there's no deadline for us."

"Fair, but I can see myself bogging down in chapter 2 as soon as things start happening."

"Like Leviticus."

Reed laughed. One year they'd tried to read through the Bible together and stalled out for weeks in Leviticus.

"All right. I'll give it a try. Switching subjects, our mail gets read."

Kathy Sue nodded.

"Suppose you hear one of the families has a problem, and you need to let me know." Reed waited a beat. "You have the cutest frown."

Kathy Sue blushed, all the more because she hadn't expected to react like that.

"We can't name names if it's sensitive."

"Right. We can use numbers for everyone. Not consecutive. Families, too."

"Can't hurt. Might help."

Reed grinned at the familiar phrase.

Then her frown came back. "Will it, though? What if I write, oh, 49 has financial problems?"

Reed frowned in turn. "Funny you should use that example. But you're right. We'll need some more numbers."

"What are the people who read the mail going to say?"

"Good question." After a couple minutes, Reed suggested, "Let's introduce it with 'Family information follows' and see if it gets left alone."

"Or 'prayer requests,' Kathy Sue suggested. "We can compare notes tomorrow night."

"Got it," Reed agreed. "So what movie is playing tonight?"

Kathy Sue laughed. "*Back to the Future III*."

* * *

Reed and Kathy Sue left the theater, arms around each other.

Kathy Sue sounded a little breathless. "How come you never introduced me to making out at the movies up-time?"

Reed chuckled. "You know as well as I do. Certain people in the church who'd hear about it and go on a tirade about the the-a-ter." He pronounced the second syllable with a long A.

Kathy Sue giggled. "Probably still will." She quickly clarified what she meant. "Not the house church. People like Deacon Underwood and Julia O'Malley."

"I can't imagine the two of them agreeing about anything."

"Oh, on the slack morals of youth, they're downright ecumenical."

Reed laughed. "You could start all sorts of trouble if you say I was studying the engine."

"Your new captain might want his own flying train."

"He definitely would. Me, too, though. If we could move supplies faster... There's got to be a way."

Kathy Sue let him think while she snuggled close.

They were most of the way home when Reed said, "Something your dad told me once. Well, probably four or five times, actually."

Kathy Sue giggled.

"The supply trucks in World War II had special routes and absolute priority on those roads. 'Nothing stops the Red Ball Express.' I need to write that down when we get home. We don't have the trucks for it, but we've got wagons and trains."

"I saw an ad for steam cars," Kathy Sue offered.

"No objection, but the cost will probably get us. We need civilians to be early adopters and drive the price down. Same with new rifles, really."

"Don't take too long writing down your plan to win the war. Although, if it'll win the war and get you home..."

"I hear that." Reed's arm tightened around Kathy Sue.

The house was dark. Anna Maria, Magdalena, and Rosina had already gone to bed.

Reed went straight to the kitchen table and wrote down his thoughts. Red Ball. Priority transportation. Horses and wagons switching teams like the Pony Express. Trains. TacRail. One-way routes where it mattered.

"I'm not really sure what the Oberpfalz is like," Reed muttered.

"Ask NESS. They were just there. We can stop by their office tomorrow."

"You are the best, Sugar."

Kathy Sue smiled, then just stood there a moment. "It's so quiet."

Reed crossed the room to the wall-mounted telephone. "No note."

"One of the girls would have made sure we found a message," Kathy Sue agreed.

"I'm sure Mom's delighted to have little kids around again for one night. She'll probably be happy to give them back tomorrow."

"Do you want us to see you off at Camp Saale Wednesday?" Kathy Sue asked.

"Yeah. Yeah, I'd like that, Sugar."

"Ok, I'll call Blackshire Elementary tomorrow and let them know Lydia will miss at least part of Wednesday."

"I'll get home as soon as I can, and we can spend time with the kids," Reed said.

"That sounds wonderful. But since they're not here tonight..."

Neustatter's European Security Services
Tuesday, March 25, 1636

Neustatter concluded a serious discussion outside with, "The Bavarian cavalry is foraging. You'll need repeaters."

"Three up-time rifles, and everyone has SRGs," Reed said. "But the MPs have Sharps carbines."

"Good. Roughly comparable to the Suhl Inc. M1635, which I understand was based on a Remington. Roughly comparable." Neustatter held up a hand. "Up-timers can argue guns like theology. Got no problem with who follows Paul or Apollos or Browning or Glock. The Sharps and the M1635 are both better than an SRG caplock, neither as good as a twentieth-century battle rifle. Stay together, support each other, and if you get hit while transporting weapons—use 'em all."

"Understood."

* * *

Inside, Astrid looked over Kathy Sue's lists.

"You are correct. These are very much like the lists I mentioned." Astrid smiled. "I will be more careful in the future—as you are."

"What do you mean?"

"These are incomplete. I see only people whose circumstances I already know or could reasonably guess."

Kathy Sue flushed slightly.

"Need to know—*und* I do not." Astrid made a few suggestions as to the best way to cross-reference the information.

Kathy Sue studied Astrid for a moment. "Is there anything you would like to do, be more involved with, in the house church?"

Astrid leaned back in her chair. "From your husband's sermon yesterday and from watching up-timers in general, I think 'Will you serve?' could soon change to 'Will you lead?'"

Kathy Sue grinned back with genuine humor. "You have us figured out. Seriously, though..."

"I keep watch of Regina, Sarah, and the *Bibelgesellschaft* girls," Astrid allowed. "If they had two or three friends with them, I could handle it. Or

Barbara and I could, perhaps. But I have heard stories of up-time youth groups, and, well, Kathy Sue, you will have teenagers long before I will. I have no desire to start early."

Kathy Sue laughed.

* * *

While the kids napped that afternoon, Kathy Sue created a master list of the men in Reed's unit. She added the information Reed had shared with her as well as what she knew of those who attended the house church. She saw the first connection: Private Jürgen Drese occasionally attended Reed's services. His wife Anna Margaretha occasionally attended the house church. The Dreses were short on money. It sounded familiar.

Kathy Sue found Jürgen's squad leader. Bruce Reynolds. That gave her a pretty shrewd notion as to how the Dreses ended up short of money. Following Astrid's advice, she reached for another sheet of paper.

Does Private Jürgen Drese spend too much money partying with Bruce Reynolds?

Private Matthias Häusser's family needed housing. They were...in Magdeburg.

Who do I contact about family needs in Magdeburg?

Private Christoph Weissensee's parents liked to check up on him. A note in Reed's handwriting appeared below.

Do not use the words helicopter parents. I do not want to explain what a helicopter is and why we aren't building them. Chris is a good kid, but they'll bug you non-stop.

Kathy Sue saw they lived in Commerce, the new planned community over in the northern lobe of West Virginia County. She'd never been over there and wasn't sure she believed the rumor Commerce might come to rival Grantville in population. She also wasn't sure how the seventeenth century had produced a pair of helicopter parents, but Reed's note made it clear she'd find out soon enough.

She put the lists away when the kids woke up.

* * *

"Daddy!Daddy!Daddy!" The older kids barreled down the hall when Reed arrived home.

Reed bent down to absorb and return hugs from Lydia, Tommy, and Mark. Once he'd extracted himself, he hung his uniform coat in one of the front closets and tugged off his boots.

Kathy Sue and Mary approached at a sedate pace.

"Sort of feel like Mr. Rogers."

Kathy Sue giggled. "On one of my 'days off,' I'll look around for a red sweater." She held up Mary. "Mary, who is that? Daddy. Da-da."

Mary looked at Reed but didn't say anything.

"Anything you want from Bavaria?"

Kathy Sue stepped close and kissed Reed. "You back safe." She was pretty sure the kids' eeewwws covered her whisper.

"Roger that."

After dinner, Anna Maria offered, "We'll go upstairs."

"No," Reed said. "We don't want to kick you out. You live here."

The ladies settled down in front of the television while Reed, Kathy Sue, and the kids attempted a board game. The kids quickly lost interest and turned to blocks.

"Weren't these blocks in Tommy and Mark's room a few days ago?" Reed asked.

"Yeah," Kathy Sue confirmed. "They migrate."

"Do you kids want to finish the game?"

Tommy shook his head. "I want real candy, not game candy. When I grow up, I'm going to make candy."

Mark's head came up from stacking blocks. "Candy?"

"Do we have any candy, Mommy?" Lydia asked.

"I don't think so, but I'll check."

Kathy Sue tried to unobtrusively return to her spot on the floor a few minutes later, but Tommy turned to her.

"Did you find any candy, Mommy?"

"No, we're all out."

"When I grow up, I'm going to make candy," Tommy announced. "Lots and lots."

Kathy Sue exchanged a look with Reed.

"Good idea," Reed said.

"We had a kind of candy called chocolate once at Gramma's," Lydia said. "It's yummy."

Kathy Sue caught herself tearing up and felt Reed squeeze her hand.

"I don't know how much chocolate there is here down-time."

"No, here isn't down-time." Lydia was insistent. "There was up-time, and there was down-time but now it's new-time. We learned it at school."

Kathy Sue saw Reed's expression and almost laughed.

"Is that a thing?" he asked.

"I guess? Maybe it's a we-live-together-now thing?" Kathy Sue wondered. "Ladies?"

Once she'd explained the question, Rosina answered. "It depends on whom you talk to. People put NTL after the date for the new timeline, but we often say you up-timers came down-time."

"*Ja*, this isn't really down-time anymore," Magdalena agreed. "It is like your up-time *melting pot*."

"Got it. Thanks," Reed said. "I should probably stop and think about that more often."

"Kids, when I can, I'll see what I can find out about chocolate," Kathy Sue told them. "Maybe someone can make it, maybe they can't. Maybe they can, but it costs more money than we want to spend."

"Are you going to be a detective, Mommy?" Lydia asked.

"What's 'tective?" Mark asked.

"A detective finds things. Or finds people, sometimes."

"I wanna do that!" Mark exclaimed.

"We can find chocolate!" Tommy added.

"Okay, candy detectives—and Lydia Bunny Rabbit—time for bed. Let's clean up."

After picking up, pajamas, bathroom, and brushing teeth, they gathered in the boys' room for story time and prayers. Once the kids were tucked in, Reed looked at Kathy Sue.

"Do you want to step out on the porch?"

Her face lit up. "We haven't done that since...I don't know when."

"It's been a while. Since before I went off to Wismar."

Kathy Sue told Magdalena, Rosina, and Anna Maria she and Reed would be outside, then they found shoes and coats.

They held hands on the porch for a couple minutes. Kathy Sue looked up at the sky.

"Oh, wow! Look, Reed."

A slightly gibbous moon shone through broken clouds. Kathy Sue led Reed down the front steps, out into their yard. They stood there and admired the night sky.

"I'm a sucker for moonlight and scattered clouds," Reed said. "It always reminds me God is up to something. Maybe it's the covers of those Peretti books you got me in high school." After a moment, he added, "Kinda dopey, I guess."

"It's not dopey at all," Kathy Sue countered. "God's up to a lot of things. People used to say, 'The Lord is moving.' That always sounded so bland. I'm glad C. S. Lewis changed it to 'on the move.'"

"Much better," Reed agreed.

"Jesus, help us understand what you want us to do," Kathy Sue said.

"Amen."

After a moment, Reed said, "I'll let you know if He drops a plan in my lap."

"I'll keep you up to date on the conference the Brethren teens are planning," Kathy Sue said.

After a few more minutes, Reed pulled Kathy Sue close. They kissed.

A few minutes later, Kathy Sue felt a little breathless. And cold. "This is wonderful, but it's more wonderful in the summer."

"Yep. Got anything you want to talk about out here, Sugar?"

"Nope. We've had the what-if-something-happens talk a few times, and I don't think anything's changed."

"Just checking."

"Which is good. But let's stick with Plan A: Don't die."

"Roger that. How 'bout you?"

"Same plan," Kathy Sue told her husband. "Don't die. No changes to Plan B or Plan C."

"I know something else isn't likely, but..."

Kathy Sue smiled. "I know you don't have any control over your schedule, but next time if you're in Grantville during the right week, we'll have a much better chance of baby number five."

Reed grimaced. "Yeah."

Kathy Sue spoke softly. "Don't worry about it. I figure we've got 'til 1646 or so. Time for three or four more. I like being a mom."

"I wish I were here with you, doing a better job of being a dad. Getting called Dada by Mary."

Kathy Sue hugged Reed. "What you're doing needs doing, and you're good at it. So leave that thought out here."

"Yes, ma'am."

She poked him in the ribs. "Don't 'ma'am' me. That's as bad as deaconess."

Reed smirked. Kathy Sue playfully shook a finger at him, because she knew he was thinking about doing it again.

After a moment, he asked, "Anything you want to leave out here?"

Kathy Sue shrugged. "Sure. Uncertainty. The days where I question whether I'm any good at this mom thing."

"You're really good at it, Kathy Sue."

"Aww. Thanks. This week the kids haven't had an off day. Barely a tussle. But sometimes..."

"Like the days I wonder if I'm getting through to any of my guys at all."

"Yeah."

"All that stays out here, too."

"Done." Kathy Sue took Reed's hands. "Lord Jesus, please help us not take any of this stuff back in the house."

"Thank You for Kathy Sue. Thank You for each of the kids. If You think we're ready for another one..."

"Thank You for Reed. Please keep him safe. Amen." Kathy Sue looked up at Reed. "Thanks for suggesting this. I feel so much lighter."

Reed scooped her up. "Yep."

Kathy Sue giggled as Reed carried her up the steps and into the house.

Wednesday, March 26, 1636

Reed awoke first and lay there a few minutes just watching Kathy Sue, who was cuddled up against him.

This has been a really nice week, God. Thank You.

* * *

Kathy Sue heard the alarm and did not want to get up.

'Morning, Lord Jesus. Thanks for everything. This is the best week of the year.

She was nice and warm next to Reed. She leaned back, reached, and smacked the right button. So far, the snooze function was surviving the seventeenth century.

"Mm, didn't miss that," Reed muttered. "'Morning, Sugar."

* * *

Kathy Sue arrived in the kitchen and hung back a couple minutes to watch daddy-daughter time as Reed got Mary to eat some porridge.

After a few bites, she shook her head. "Milk, Dada!"

"Aw."

Kathy Sue teared up and wiped her eyes in annoyance.

Reed's head came around. "Sugar?"

"Hey there. You guys look like you're enjoying breakfast."

"Enjoying it, wearing it... I got a 'dada.' How are you doing?"

"I just had a moment. I promise I won't lose it. Not 'til we get home."

"Oh, Sugar." Reed got up and embraced Kathy Sue. "It sucks."

"Yeah. It does. It's gonna have to wait, though. We've got stuff to do."

Camp Saale

Reed moved along the long lines of wagons drawn up between the rows of barracks and former barracks. They'd loaded the wagons over the last couple days, and shifts of MPs stood guard over them. This morning the men hitched up the teams. Many were oxen, but some were draft horses. Most of the military police company escorting them was mounted. The wagons were covered, and the whole column seemed right out of a western.

Might be the real reason we haven't been able to raise many cavalry units, Reed reflected. *Supply is a priority.*

He paused here and there to check a wagon's load, tug on a rope with the requisite, "That's not going anywhere," and assess whether the men were ready. Then he gathered them for Captain Stauttenbecker.

"Men, just like we briefed. The infantry who trained here in '33 marched north along the railroad and stopped for the night in the railroad construction camps. Same for us, but we're headed south. *Erster Leutnant* Burroughs explained why we do it this way.

"We will stop at the gate. Those of you with families here will have a chance to say goodbye, but no more than ten minutes. We have a lot of ground to cover today."

* * *

Kathy Sue watched the wagons roll to the gate. Then soldiers dismounted.

"Look, there's Daddy." Kathy Sue crouched down and pointed. Then, she grabbed both Tommy and Mark as they tried to run toward him.

"Stop! Boys, we do not run at horses. We have to be careful, like we are around cars and trains."

Reed dismounted and handed the reins to a soldier staying by the wagon. *One of the new men who came down from Magdeburg*, Kathy Sue surmised.

"Daddy!" Lydia exclaimed. "You have a horse!"

"The Army has horses, and they let me ride them."

"Can we have a ride? Can we?"

"We can't right now," Reed answered. "We're about to leave."

"Can we pet the horse?"

Reed exchanged glances with Kathy Sue. "One at a time?"

She nodded.

"Okay, we'll take turns. Everybody else stay with Mommy."

Reed's horse was only marginally interested in the small humans petting it.

Reed hugged each of the kids.

"Everybody hold hands," Kathy Sue directed. "Dear Jesus, please keep Daddy safe."

"Lord, please watch over Kathy Sue and Lydia, Tommy, Mark, and Mary. Amen."

"Write lots," Kathy Sue requested. "Let me know if you need anything sent."

"Will do."

Reed pulled Kathy Sue close, and they kissed.

"I love you."

"I love you."

"Ew."

Kathy Sue saw Lydia try to cover her brothers' eyes.

"See you all later," Reed said. He stepped back and mounted his horse. "Fifty-First Supply! Mount up!"

He and Bruce Reynolds rode the line, making sure everyone was in place. Then he reported to Captain Stauttenbecker.

"The company is ready, sir!"

"Move out!"

Kathy Sue and the kids watched Reed and the others ride out of Camp Saale.

"Mommy," Tommy said. "I'm sad."

"I know, buddy. So am I. I think everyone is. You can say hi to the other kids, and then we'll drop Lydia off at school."

Minutes later, Kathy Sue was deep in conversation with fellow military wives who raised a whole additional set of questions and issues. Some of them fought back tears with varying levels of success. She saw Tommy go up to a boy who was crying and give him a hug.

The first few days are really hard, but we're going to make it. "Can I tell you about the first time Reed went off to the war? Back in '31?"

She saw a mixture of relief and expectation on their faces.

Yeah, we got this.

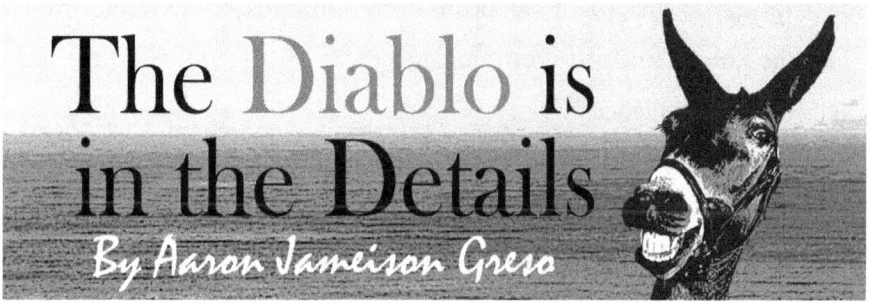

The Diablo Is In The Details

Aaron Jameison Greso

Venice

Late May 1634

Zuan, the pilot boat's oarsman, kept smiling as he bobbed his head. "They were standing in a line outside the door of the new CPE embassy. I'd swear to it."

"Why would anyone stand in line to buy a compass?" The Portuguese merchant-captain, Roberto, asked that just as Francesco, the Venetian port pilot, politely nudged the captain aside to grab the boat's tie-rope.

"There is no reason for me to buy some fancy compass 'from the future.' I always know where I'm going." Francesco grabbed the rope. "But I wouldn't mind having that huge black jackass you've got on deck. It must be worth a fortune. Why else would a knight make such an effort to groom it?"

"That knight's name is Antonio. Some corsairs had it in for him off Sicily," said Roberto. "The Maltese Brethren said the recovering knight raised it from a sick foal and they just up and gave it to him. They asked me to look after the knight and be his friend until his jack sells tomorrow."

As the knight stopped grooming and came out from behind the jack, there was a long silence.

Francesco thumped into the rowboat. "Come on, Zuan, we are off to Venice to announce the sale of a huge Maltese jack. His knight is going to need all the help and ducats he can get."

* * *

After a brief discussion the following morning, at the strong behest of the knight, Roberto and Antonio took the stockyard ferry to Venice and the new CPE embassy.

* * *

"No! Out! Corporal, escort this man out the door!"

After Versteh's building-resonating outburst, an ambitious junior aide rushed in from the room's private entrance. "Sir, sir, here are the latest compass applications. The print shop won't have any more applications ready until noon. You might have time for lunch today, sir."

"Who is in line now, Kit?"

"Sir, apart from those thirty or so waiting to fill out applications at the Embassy door, four, sir. One looks like some kind of knight by his uniform."

"Before you go back up front, what is your assessment of the compass program so far?"

"The compasses are beautiful. Everyone wants one even though Corporal McKenna says the battlefield ones are better. The idea is brilliant. The USE will quickly know every merchant and captain on all of the Mediterranean coasts. When you sold the one that resold for 200 ducats, everybody started showing up. No advertising necessary."

"Next!" the buttered-up Versteh bellowed with renewed zeal.

* * *

Roberto, who had just missed being run over by the latest rush of Scots mercenaries-turned-Horse Marines, stood behind Antonio and breathed heavily. "That compass-room man is quick to anger. What do you suppose the last fellow got wrong?" said the captain.

While moving up to the compass-room door, Antonio sighed. "I think the man with the compasses simply did not like the answers the merchant gave. I have heard that when you are in there, you are asked to tell a good story and to have a good reason to buy one of those new compasses from the future.

"I have also heard that the man has sold only two of their compasses to 'true traders.' If anyone lies, the devil of a man calls out the guards. As you have just seen, it is also known that anyone arguing is also escorted out."

"Oh. Good to know. What else did you find out when I was refreshing myself?"

"Before I say anything else, my dear captain Roberto, you certainly took your time refreshing yourself. We are next, and now I won't get a chance to refresh myself. Thank you very much for not listening to me when I told you to get back quickly."

Roberto immediately redirected Antonio's rising ire. "How did you find out about the questions being asked?"

"Oh, a little angel told me," the irritated knight replied with a wry grin. "Attending mass more often would certainly help you develop such angelic listening skills."

"Ah, so you listen to angels. What else did that little angel tell you?"

"Oh, you are supposed to tell a story regarding where your trade items come from and make comments about something the inhabitants of the new future Grantville City would want to eat. This is quite odd. I believe it is a trick question. I am not sure how to answer such a question. Other than that, you just simply respond to questions about who you are and where you trade and how and what you trade.

"However, Roberto, this time I think you should hold back your dealing prowess and let me do the talking. This is because I have heard that even though the man actually sells compasses, he considers himself a diplomat, not a salesman to be bargained with."

Pausing to let Corporal McKenna's guards re-station themselves at the compass-room door, the chastened Portuguese captain tried to assuage the knight. "So, in the meantime, we just wait for compasses to be sold to us, yes?"

"Uh, speaking of sales," Antonio replied, "what makes you so sure your Jacques will sell my Maltese jack and your jennet asses for higher prices here?"

"Don't worry. Jacques has occasionally traded donkeys at the Venetian coast corral for at least two years. The Maltese Brethren say he always picks his jacks and jennets to command the best prices. And the jennets will easily sell for more when he tells buyers that they are already well endowed by a handsome jack."

"NEXT!"

With Antonio's confidence up to the standard of any knight, he and Roberto nodded to each other and walked into the compass room with McKenna and waited.

* * *

After McKenna had left, Versteh finished writing a quick summary of the previous interview and looked up. A Portuguese knight and what looks to be a Portuguese captain. Hm. It is good to have an unusual combination for a change. Either one of these two might actually engage in trade and actually want to keep and use a compass. I hope they give me some good information.

As usual, to display his verbal prowess, Versteh introduced himself in loud English. "Gentlemen, I am called Versteh, and I assume you can understand what I am saying. So, I will ask you a few questions before proceeding to the compasses. The first question is: Do you know what electricity is and from where it comes?"

A moment after Antonio translated the best he could for Roberto, both men shook their heads from side to side. Because this was a trick question, Versteh was somewhat impressed with the honest response. Electricity was common knowledge only to Grantville citizens. Most interviewees had made up an answer but these two men did not. Oh, we may have honest traders this time.

"Gentlemen, the second question is: Do you know what chocolate is and from where it comes?"

After another pause, Versteh saw the knight slowly shake his head but the captain held up his hand as he nudged the knight aside.

Following a quick translation of Roberto's comments, Antonio replied to Versteh, "Is it not possible to make sweetened cacao into a chocolate drink with cane sugar? Cacao beans have just started trading in the Azores. They come from Tierra Firme. Sugar comes from there, or thereabouts, but sugar cane also grows near Africa on the island of Madeira from where the captain trades."

Antonio's brief answer was the best response regarding chocolate Versteh had heard. However, Versteh had to quickly substitute an eager reply with a dull demeanor to maintain his composure. "Ah, that is interesting. Have either of you ever traded for chocolate?"

After another short discussion between the knight and the captain, Antonio pointed to Roberto and replied, "No, but he would like to."

"Sehr gut," said Versteh. The men had passed two of Versteh's important preliminary screening test questions.

"Gentlemen, to receive a Grantville compass, you will need to pay 20 ducats apiece, and you will only be able to obtain one each. However, a few more questions are required. First, did you bring payments with you?"

Both Roberto and Antonio showed their purses.

Versteh shoved their newly proffered ducats under his desk. Holding payments hostage prompted better answers to more difficult questions.

"Gentlemen, before you receive your compasses, you will now please tell me a little more about yourselves. You will do so by answering the following questions. What are your names, why are you worthy of such names, and why are you trading in Venice?"

The two exchanged words, and Antonio spoke up after again pointing to the captain. "He is Roberto Columbus. He is related to Christopher Columbus, discoverer of the New World. He trades the renowned Madeira wine. The Portuguese captain trades between Funchal, the Azores, and the Canaries. Sometimes he trades with Sicily, Malta, and Venice. He is a skilled captain, he is shrewd beyond compare, and could sell a cross to a Turk if he were given half a chance.

"Today we trade Madeira wine for lumber as well as selling Maltese jacks and jennets. At the moment, we are trading a precious fourteen-hand jack who is just now becoming well-known throughout the Mediterranean.

"I am Antonio of the house de Souza. I am a Portuguese knight and while serving in the coast guard and off the waters of West Africa, I and those I commanded sunk many pirate vessels."

To this last remark, Versteh softly replied, "Huh, I see."

During Versteh's brief response, Antonio watched Versteh's eyes look toward what had once been the knight's arm. "Do not let this mark of bravery discourage you. I am respected among my fellow sailors for fighting corsairs."

Antonio deflected Versteh's uneasiness from his missing arm. "But now, mein Herr, please tell us about yourself. Tell us why you are worthy of your name. Then, if you may, please tell us about this embassy and Grantville."

This time, Versteh's skepticism changed to enthusiasm. This was a new level of information exchange. After Versteh instructed the corporal to close the door, he began.

"I am Versteh Himmelmann, and I am a two-year graduate of Grantville's highest school. I have been in Venice since the start of the embassy here. In an advanced Grantville class, I learned about Maltese jacks and how they were given to George Washington to help breed the most prestigious mules that helped settle the new world.

"I am well versed in Grantville City history, activities and trade practices near Grantville, Magdeburg, and..."

While Versteh plowed on, Roberto whispered to Antonio, "Who is George Washington?"

"Shh," Antonio whispered back. "Shut up and listen. Be polite and maybe he will change his mind and sell us another compass."

* * *

"...as for electricity, well, if there is a will, there is a way...and I have read all about chocolate and how it is made into an edible bar and that it tastes fabulous...and because I understand most languages in the Germanies, I am called Versteh which, in German, means 'understand.' Although I am not fluent in Portuguese yet...and so this leads me to ask, why do you want these compasses?"

Trying in vain to shorten the conversation and keep Antonio in dry trousers, Roberto quickly replied, once the knight had translated: "Oh, a captain or a knight knows the value of a compass. They are also useful when trying to explain directions to other crewmen or common traders who still court danger navigating by following a shoreline. We are finished now, yes?"

* * *

Later, while Versteh continued to extol his virtues, Corporal McKenna quietly propped open the door, entered the room, and smiled sympathetically at the fidgeting knight's inability to conceal his "lack-of-refreshment discomfort." The corporal then gave Versteh the "long line" warning by standing at attention and staring at Versteh while waiting for the aide to stop talking and acknowledge his presence.

* * *

During yet another translation to Roberto, and just as the corporal was pointing out the door and trying to get Versteh's attention, Antonio also looked at the long line. "Excuse me, Herr Versteh, but would you like to join us for the midday meal? Our expense, of course, but you would be welcome to choose where we go."

"Indeed, most certainly! Oh my, but first, here are your compasses." Versteh took two boxed compasses from under his desk and handed them to the captain and knight, along with their purses. "Follow me, gentlemen."

Versteh exhaled slowly at the line of merchants. "Pardon me, gentlemen, some other time perhaps. The embassy's mission comes first." Versteh shook hands with the new compass owners.

* * *

Versteh started in on his interview notes. This time, however, there was a bit more of a determined smile as he thought.

Hmmm, the compasses will pay for themselves by just providing trade contacts. This modern process of trading inferior products for information must have been of great value to people living in the future. I must see these gentlemen again. I can't imagine the questions I could ask.

* * *

While Versteh contemplated Grantville policy with McKenna, Roberto turned his head and smiled at Antonio as they hustled past the line of merchantmen.

"Nice job, Antonio. Versteh couldn't possibly go to lunch. You saw and used the long line as an excuse to help us escape that exasperating, semi-merchant diplomat. Now hurry up. You will need to refresh yourself. This way."

* * *

Antonio and Roberto arrived at the stockyard in good spirits. Roberto had made a generous profit from the cargo of Madeira and Maltese jennets while also acquiring a good supply of excellent lumber. However, Antonio was dismayed when he found out his jack had not sold.

* * *

For a long moment Jacques just kept slowly shaking his head until he said, "The crowd was too large. They were all trying to touch and prod him. The mob kept crowding around while the jack ran around inside the corral until he suddenly stopped and lifted his muzzle into the air. Nothing but quiet followed when everybody else looked up and stuck their noses into the air.

"He broke through the corral and ended up going after a mare that had just come into the stockyard. After helping him up, I convinced the young man riding the mare that he would be blessed with a new, superior mule in a year—for no stud cost. The man was not badly hurt so he agreed. However, the man's father, being one of the biggest mule breeders around, made sure nobody else bought the jack by calling it 'The Diablo.' He kept saying it would curse anyone who touched it.

"Sirs, who wants to buy the Diablo? At least the young man's father bought all our well-endowed jennets.

"It is that jack's lot in life to wander forth with just one reason. After that Diablo sated his desire, he just wandered back to the corral as though nothing had happened. All the while, the mare and the jennets ran as far away from him as they could.

"Unfortunately, that jackass will damage anything that gets between him and any mare or jennet. He is too amorous. By the way, captain, the stockyard filed a lien on your ship for damages."

"Ah," sighed the captain. "No profit on him. Antonio, the brothers on Malta warned me that could happen. Sicilian ports are more ruthless with liens. That's why I didn't try to sell your Diablo till Venice."

Roberto then chuckled. "The brothers might take your Diablo back when we deliver our lumber—as long as nobody says anything about what happened here."

"He raises havoc everywhere except when we are at sea. They won't take him back. What do you think I should do, Roberto?"

Roberto looked at the concern on Antonio's face while taking note of the knight's missing arm.

"Antonio, when you lost your arm, the Maltese Brethren and you both knew you would never be preferred for knight service again. When I was in Malta, I talked with the brother who carried you to his monastery after you were horribly wounded. That brother knew you would need to leave Malta and find a better future. He knew that raising an ass, and selling it, would take you beyond Malta, yes?

"Just like Versteh, you are more than what others think you are. Antonio, you may have learned how to raise a Diablo but you should remember you are still a knight. Your work on Malta brought you back to health and has now brought you back to the sea. Still, you are not happy even if an angel occasionally gives you a reason to smile, yes? I know quite a few more earthly angels in Portugal that could do that."

"I am not a lusty Diablo, Roberto."

"Ah, but maybe you need to have something to lust for, eh? You should try to find some chocolate to eat. Did not Versteh say Grantville people think chocolate tastes fabulous? Perhaps you and I were meant to trade that jack across the ocean for cacao beans? Do not worry. We will take the ass to Portugal with us if the brothers will not have him."

"Roberto, how do you know all this?"

"Antonio, I do not listen to the angels the way you do, but I listen to what many merchants talk about." Roberto's teeth showed in a salesman's seasoned smile.

"That Diablo knows when a jennet or mare is ready so he can be first. We also have a great opportunity to be first to sell Grantville all the cacao or chocolate they want. And we will get top price for selling such a high-demand product—without requiring any middlemen. All we have to do is make sure we are first to deliver and to do so before the opportunity disappears. Just like the way that Diablo goes after jennets and mares—before they run away, yes?

"Antonio, just like your Diablo, perhaps you should think about what you should do first for your future. Besides, that Diablo of yours has always followed his own compass. Perhaps now it is time for you to follow yours?"

Emancipation and Education

Terry Howard

Grantville

September 1636

Reverend Mary Ellen Jones had a dilemma. It was Wednesday evening after the midweek service and choir practice, early in September 1636. A nervous young man named William Schmid was waiting until he could speak to her alone.

"Reverend Jones, I need your assistance. I have been told that a suit with the courts for emancipation has a much better chance of success if I have my pastor's support."

Mary Ellen was shocked. William was not one of the wild ones. He was quiet, stayed out of trouble, and got good grades. Mary Ellen did not approve of children severing the legal ties that bound a family together.

"Why do you want to do that, William?" Mary Ellen asked.

The Schmid family was not the most regular in attendance, but they seemed nice enough. The father did not have a reputation for domestic violence—which was the most common reason she could think of for a child to sue for emancipation.

"You see, Pastor, Papa wants me to quit school and get a job. I will be sixteen late this month, and I've finished up the eighth-grade curriculum. It's not that I'm not working. I push one of the McAdams delivery carts before school."

The carts delivered newspapers, eggs, milk, and bread. They kept the routes short enough that the delivery guys could get to school on time. "But Papa says I need a real job since at sixteen the local law will let me do so."

"You can't work in the coal mine until you're eighteen and have a diploma," Mary Ellen pointed out.

"I tried that argument. Papa said I could make a lot of money in the four years it will take to finish high school. I need to grow up and get a job."

"But the delivery carts don't pay well enough to pay rent and eat. The court will want to see that you are self-supporting. Let me talk to your father," Mary suggested.

* * *

"Pastor Jones." William's father was adamant. "The boy needs to grow up and get a job. Anywhere else in the world, he'd already be working."

"But he can get a much better job with a high school diploma," Mary Ellen said.

"If the boy wants to get more education, let him take night school classes. He needs to get on with his life, start saving money to get married someday."

"But with a high school diploma, he can get a job at the mine. The jobs he can get at his age will hardly pay for rent and groceries."

"That's four years thrown away. He can get an apprenticeship at the tannery and learn a trade." The tannery was mostly worked by convict laborers. Any sentence over ninety days could be served on the county road gang. For anything longer than that, you went to work at the tannery. The rooms were spartan, the food plain, and the company was questionable. True, it was a trade, and they did take apprentices. But that was all you could say about it.

"Let him be a man, get a job, and get on with his life," Papa Schmid said. "If he's staying under my roof at his age then he's working full time. Period."

"So, you don't mind if he goes to school as long as he moves out?" Mary Ellen asked.

"If he can make a living and still go to school then he's a man, and that's a man's business."

* * *

Mary Ellen told William the next evening. "We've got until your birthday at the end of the month to find someone who can use some live-in help, or you are looking at an apprenticeship at the tannery. I've checked with Mr. Kindred. He doesn't have a spare bedroom and doesn't need any more help. Any ideas?"

"One," William said, "But Papa will throw a fit. I've talked to Pastor Green. That's why I need to be emancipated. When we were Lutherans, the pastor preached against the Anabaptists. Papa doesn't care much about religion. But when we were Catholics, they preached against them too. So did the Calvinists. It seems to be the only thing they agree on is that they are each the one true church and that everybody else is wrong, especially the Anabaptists. That is why we ended up being Methodist when we came here. Papa was fed up with changing religion every time the ruler died, and the religion changed with the new heir. Since you weren't Catholic, Calvinist, or Lutheran, he thought you would be different. But he's sure the Anabaptists are all anarchists and antichrists or madmen like the Münster Anabaptists. Troublemakers, out to tear the world down. He thinks the Baptists are just a different name for Anabaptists who survived until up-time and were brought back with Grantville. He points out that the madmen of Münster wanted everything to be held in common, like Green is doing with the farm."

"Well, he is partially correct. They share a lot of ideas, but there's a lot of influence from English Nonconformists, too. Green and his lot up on the mountain are good people. As are Underwood and the old Southern Baptists. The down-time group here in town are solid people. Not radicals like the Münster group was."

"Well, I've checked with the Holiday Lodge since they have live-in help, and they want you to be eighteen. Most places in town want you to be eighteen for full-time employment. Part-time after school won't help. Papa is insistent that I must have a full-time job. I've talked to Pastor Green. If I agree to the work schedule that the school kids follow and set up a serious study program, he'll let me stay at the college and go to high school. That is if I'm emancipated first. Papa sure won't allow it. And if I have your support. Green doesn't want to be accused of stealing children or stealing sheep."

Mary Ellen laughed. "He considers us to be reformed, schismatic, Catholic separatists. And he's right, if you concede that the Church of England are English Catholic separatists."

"But if I'm not clear through the courts, Papa will insist that I come home, afraid that I'll become a madman of Münster, under their influence. Then he's got the job lined up for me at the tannery.

That is why I need your help. Being an apprentice tanner is like being a convict. Green's program will teach me a trade, like printing or making steam engines. Or bookbinding. While studying—and farming, which they all help with. Even Green himself."

"Yes," Mary Ellen said, "he is known for that. Everyone works at farming when the need comes up. While doing something else. Mostly having to do with printing odd books that have a limited market."

"Still," William said, "they eat well, and the younger ones get to go to school full time. I guess I can handle learning Greek and Hebrew on top of doing homework for high school. Anna from Liverpool doesn't seem to be put out with it. She came with her brother. It would be a full twelve-hour day but so would tanning leather—and I'd be getting an education in the Bible from a Baptist viewpoint. Which won't kill me."

"William, I am usually not in favor of someone becoming an emancipated minor. But if the alternative is working at the tannery or working on a farm while going to high school and getting a Bible college education from Doctor Green, I'll go to court for you."

* * *

Mary Ellen sat in chambers with the judge, Maurice Tito. "I'm mostly against minor emancipation. But in this case, William wants to stay in high school, and his father wants him to go to work at the tannery. Doctor Green has agreed to take the boy on as a Bible student and let him go to high school. His father will object. In his opinion, all Anabaptists are like the madmen of Münster. So, we need the boy free and clear, or he could end up at the tannery."

"I see," Maurice said. "Well, wanting to stay in high school is laudable. But does the boy know just how much work goes into running a farm?"

"He's had long conversations with a girl from the farm. Did you know that Doctor Green insists on working the farm four hours a day while teaching a full program? He teaches that the priesthood of all believers means that anyone who shares in the benefits should also share in the labor."

"Well, I don't see any reason not to grant it. He has an address, an income, and a long-term strategy for his future."

Each day of the week before his birthday William sent a parcel of clothing and possessions up to the farm with Anna. Instead of going home Friday after school, he went up to the farm where the ladies had made him a birthday cake to welcome him to the community.

* * *

When he did not come home at the end of the day, his father went to the police. "I need you to do something about the Anabaptists up on the mountain."

At the word Anabaptist, the police officer behind the counter grew cautious. Religion was a touchy subject before the law.

"They've kidnaped my son. I want him back."

"Have you received a ransom note?"

"No. He's under a spell and won't come home. I think that girl from England has him enchanted."

"We'll send someone up there to see what is going on."

When Lyndon Johnson came back down from the Anabaptist college farm he went to see

William Schmid's father.

"Herr Schmid, I've talked to William. He said he's staying at the farm."

"He's my son and he will come home." Herr Schmid started screaming about kidnapping and witchcraft and spells.

Lyndon said, "I talked to the judge. He said you wanted the boy to quit school. Green will let him stay in school and graduate. So he agreed to the emancipation if William moves to the farm."

"That is just not right."

"Sir, it is perfectly legal."

"Taking children away from their parents isn't right."

"Making him quit school isn't right, either."

"I want to keep him safe from those people."

"He wants to finish high school."

"And waste the next four years of his life when he could be making a living and learning a trade."

"The farm will teach him a trade." Lyndon said.

"Preaching heresy is not a trade."

"Bookbinding or printing is."

"But preaching heresy comes with it."

"I've talked to Reverend Mrs. Jones. She doesn't think that Green is a heretic."

"Because she is one herself. What business does a woman have being a preacher? She's not Lutheran or Catholic or Reformed. They don't allow women to be preachers."

"She and her husband are Methodists. The Methodists are a very respected religion up-time."

"I want my son back home."

"So you can send him to the tannery."

"It's a trade."

"And up on the mountain, he will learn a trade. He might even become an engineer and learn to make steam engines."

"What he will learn is heresy and how to please that girl from England. I want my son back."

"So you can send him away to make leather?"

"At least he'd be safe from those mad men of Münster."

"Herr Schmid, the judge has granted him his freedom. I'm afraid that there is nothing I can do, and that there is no way you can make him come home. I've looked into it, and everything is perfectly legal. The boy is there of his own free will, and everything is in order. If there isn't anything else, then have a good day."

Herr Schmid screamed about the Anabaptist kidnapping, casting spells, and corrupting the youth of the town for months on end.

William spent that Saturday with the rest of the school kids out on the mountainside picking raspberry leaves for raspberry mint tea, as Mabel Jenkins' recipe book said the best time of the year to harvest them was after the berry crop was done and before the first frost. William and Mary found some quiet time alone on the mountainside while picking raspberry leaves.

Stilettos, Part 2
Bethanne Kim

*I*n up-time West Virginia, a stiletto was a type of women's shoe with an exceptionally high, exceedingly thin heel. By 2000, most people had forgotten the 1950s origins of the name. Stiletto high heels were named for a specific type of Italian knife with an unusually long, thin blade and a pointed tip–ideal for stabbing. By the 1950s, they were normally automatic or switchblade knives, but in the 1630s, they were fixed blades that lacked a true cutting edge. Stiletto knives are intended as thrusting weapons, not slicing ones, and had their origins with knights who used them to finish off fallen or injured enemies and are particularly associated with Sicily.

Any down-timers who were familiar with a "stiletto" would know it as this type of knife, one destined to be a favorite of assassins because of its lethality and ease of concealment, not as a shoe. Part 1 of this story established both these points, and that up-time girls were interested in both kinds of stilettos, if they were available to buy.

Sicily, Mercantolo Home
August 1636

"Mother." Cristoforo Mercantolo's acid tone matched his scowl as he pushed open the ornately decorated wooden door and entered their sparsely decorated but immaculately clean home.

Looking up from the shirt she was mending, Vittoria cocked her head. *That must be a letter from Scipione. Only our son can make Cristoforo that cross. Even when he is many weeks' journey away from us!* "Yes, Father?"

"Your son would like us to send him two dozen stilettos."

Her squint returned and intensified as Vittoria scrunched the shirt into her balled fists. "How does he think we can pay for twenty-four knives? And why would he need so many? I was promised that Grantville would be safe. Are there so many battles happening in Grantville? We are not sacrificing to send him to Grantville to play the fool."

Focused on the letter again, Scipione "Skip" Mercantolo's father waved a second piece of paper in the air with his free hand. "Scipione sent money. He says he has eight orders from people in Grantville, two more possible orders, and others like the knife he has shown them. Once they see what we send, he expects more orders." He looked up. "That is where the money came from. The people who have already ordered gave him half of the money up front."

Sniff. "We never should have sent him to that place. They don't even use his real name!" *Sniff.* "'Skip' is not a name." *Sniff.* "Does that money even cover the materials needed to make so many knives? What about the cost for the smith? What nonsense!" Vittoria shook out the shirt she had been abusing. A snapping sound filled the air as she prepared to resume her repair work.

Hopping out of her way, Cristoforo nodded along with Vittoria's words. "I had the same questions. I spoke to a bladesmith on the way home. I don't know how much we might keep but the smith confirmed Scipione definitely sent more than enough to pay for two dozen stilettos. Scipione also said he will keep part of the money from 'the next order' to pay for his room and board for the spring, so we won't need to send money. But he needs this order quickly. He claims he will get bonuses if the knives are delivered before Christmas, and that he will send the full amount of any bonuses to us."

"Before Christmas! From Sicily to the middle of Germany? Is that all? Would he like them delivered by angels who descend from a rainbow, blowing heavenly horns?"

"Ah, no. He would, if possible, like them delivered by a journeyman or new master bladesmith skilled at making stilettos and similar knives who would like to stay in Grantville to open a shop selling them."

"Where, pray tell, is the money for this business coming from?"

"He's a bit vague, but it seems that he has arranged financing in Grantville." Cristoforo shrugged. "We already know things are different there. We have heard of businesses started by *children* that have done well."

Sniff. "How does he propose we will find this journeyman or new master to make stilettos in Grantville? Really, Cristoforo, your son is being ridiculous."

Seeing the way his wife's eyes snapped, Cristoforo silently moved farther from her, sidling over enough to place a small table between them, while Vittoria resumed mending. A few minutes later, she stopped. "Alessandro."

Head bobbing down onto his chest, Cristoforo popped awake as he wiped a bit of drool from his chin. "What?"

"Alessandro is a journeyman smith. I overheard Masina and Federigo talking about his prospects. It seems the families have been negotiating for Alessandro to become betrothed to their daughter, but his prospects for having his own shop are poor. He has the skills and a completed master work, but there is not enough business for another master bladesmith here, so he has not moved quickly to finish the process. Even so, there is little left for him to do to become a master. The only thing holding him back is finding a place to go as a master. Alessandro could go to *Grantville* as a master."

Always decisive, Vittoria bit off the end of her thread and put the shirt in her mending basket. Standing, she smoothed her hair and her skirt before moving toward the door. "I will speak to everyone who needs to know and arrange his departure. What does Alessandro need to bring?"

Calvert Hill Student Housing
Early December 1636

Maria blinked in surprise. *He looks like a smith but sounds like a former choirboy. He's not bad looking.* She shook her head. *Focus!* "Excuse me?"

The man's English was halting and limited. "I look Scipione Mercantolo."

"Skip?"

The man shrugged, clearly uncertain. *"Forsi?* Scipione Mercantolo."

That accent sounds like Skip. Too bad I don't know his last name. "*Für Sie?* What do you mean it's for me? I think we need to find Skip." Maria waved for him to follow her to the third cabin in the row, then knocked on the plain wooden door. "Hello! Is Skip here?"

Skip opened the door, head turtling back in surprise. He stared at the man for a minute, eyes scanning as if searching for something. His switch to his native tongue confirmed Maria's guess. "Alessandro? Why are you here?"

"Did you not ask your parents for a journeyman or new master to make stilettos? You did! And it is me." His chest puffed out with pride, arms spread wide as if to say *ta da*! "I am the new master! You did not expect this. So, what is the plan?"

"Less a plan, more an idea."

Happy demeanor instantly gone, Alessandro grabbed the straps of his bag and moved back toward the door. "I have spent much time and money to come here. I was told there was a plan, not an 'idea.'"

Hands held up, palms out in the universal "stop" gesture, Skip stepped between Alessandro and the door, then reached out for Alessandro's bags. "Please, you must be cold. Sit and warm yourself while I explain." Briefly switching back to English, Skip turned toward Maria. "Maria, thanks for bringing Alessandro over here. My parents sent him to help me."

As Alessandro hung his coat near the door and settled himself into a chair, Skip made two steaming cups of herbal tea. When Skip finally stopped fussing like a grandmother, clearly avoiding an explanation, and settled into a chair, Alessandro thumped his mug onto the worn, but solid, side table, a small amount of tea splashing out to join the other stains. He spit out a single angry word. "Explain."

Skip sighed. *I was hoping to figure out an easy way to describe how this is a good business opportunity before someone got here.* "Up-time, in the future-that-won't-be, women wore high-heeled shoes they called stilettos. They were named for blades like the ones you make, but in the time of the Grantville that was sent back to us, stiletto blades were rare, and stiletto shoes were, well, not really common because women mostly wore them for fancy dress, but they were a lot more common than stiletto blades. The shoes had been around for decades and no one remembered where the name for the shoes came from. To up-timers, stilettos are shoes, not knives.

"So, women in Grantville thought it was funny when they found out their shoes were named for knives. And they want to buy the knives, especially to wear when they are dressed up and can only carry a very small weapon. Like a stiletto. They call it concealed carry, and all the up-timers seem to find conceal-carrying a knife named for a shoe (even though it was really the other way around) hilarious. Not many of them still want the shoes now, but a lot of them would like a small, easily concealed knife."

Rising, Alessandro paced to the window and looked toward the high school. Part of the athletic facilities were barely visible. "And who is the stranger I am to be in business with? Do they know anything about being a smith or about business? Is it another child? Traveling here, I heard about too many businesses run by children."

Alessandro might have emphasized the last word, or it might have been Skip's imagination. If Alessandro had been facing him, Skip's sudden tension and narrowed eyes would have warned him what part angered the young man. His voice ice-cold, Skip's words were clipped and hard. "I am not a child, nor am I a fool, Alessandro. I have spent years living here, learning their ways and looking, always, for the right chance to start a business."

Turning, the young master stopped and looked at the outraged young man who had brought him all this way and knew more about Grantville than anyone else Alessandro had met. Skip of Grantville, no longer truly Scipione of Sicily, was no longer the young boy Alessandro remembered. "Fair enough. I do not know Grantville and their ways as you do, and you are not a child. I must continue to trust you, for I have no other choice. Now, tell me of this new partner."

Taking a deep breath and unclenching his whole body, Skip nodded. "Helmut Förster. He's a bladesmith who moved to Grantville right after the Ring of Fire." Alessandro's confusion was plain. "I forgot, you're new here, and the English words don't mean anything to you. The Ring of Fire is what they call the big event that sent Grantville back here and created the Ring Wall around town. You may have seen it on your way here. If not, we'll go there one day when it's not so cold. That's also why it's called the Ring Wall. The moment Grantville was sent back, a giant sphere of fire surrounded the whole place. Anyhow, Master Förster has a good forge now and a few journeymen who can work with you. He doesn't have time to spend on this, but his journeymen are interested in learning how to make a new kind of blade, and he has agreed to it. It'll mean more business for them when they start their own."

Sitting again, arms crossed, legs stretched out in front of him, Alessandro leaned back in his wooden chair. "And what will he get in return?"

Skip smiled, trying to get Alessandro to relax. "You *are* new here. Yeah, a lot of people want 'a piece of the action' when they help a new business, but others want to 'give back' and help someone else. Especially if someone helped them or they got a *really* lucky break to get started. Master Förster's like that. A local business helped him get started in Grantville, then one of the kids came to him with an idea that turned into a profitable business—and Sandy really was still a kid, twelve I think, when he came up with the business idea.

"So, Master Förster is willing to help others out as a way to 'pay it forward.' In this case, it's about his journeymen, not you. He wants you to pick one, help them become a master, then bring them in as your partner to manage the local side of things."

Alessandro, who'd been thoughtfully sipping his tea, stopped, frozen, with his mug halfway back down to the table. With a quick shake of his head, his eyes refocused, and he set the mug down. "What do I get out of it and what will it cost me, beyond training one of his journeymen and accepting him as my partner?"

"The deal is that you can use his space for six months, but obviously your own tools and you pay your expenses for materials. In exchange, you teach his journeymen how to make stilettos, and let the apprentices start to learn the process. After six months, you will select a journeyman to become your partner and possibly one more who will remain a journeyman with your new business, same for apprentices. You get to pick two or three to go with you, but he'll have final approval. You start paying for the space you are using after six months, and you'll need to start looking for your own space so you can move out."

Skip sipped the still-warm tea, clearly savoring the warmth as it slid down his throat. His eyes closed briefly before he continued. "Honestly, I think you can choose apprentices from wherever you want and maybe the second journeyman. The position he really cares strongly about is the journeyman who will become a master and your partner. There are a surprising number of good master smiths here in Grantville. Master Förster giving you permission to 'poach' a few trainees is a lucky break for the new business."

Most of the tension had left Alessandro's face, but not all of it. His massive smith's muscles hadn't relaxed an iota. "What work is it they do now? And why would he let so many leave his smithy?"

Skip shrugged. "Mostly kitchen knives, I think. Master Förster used to be a military smith so he can do all kinds of larger bladed weapons, but Sandy Eckerlin got him to start making kitchen knives. The business is doing pretty well, from what I hear."

"Pah. Kitchen knives. Those are nothing special."

"*Up-time* kitchen knives. I don't know the details, but they look different and I heard Master Förster did a fair bit of research and experimenting to get them right. If things don't work out and you go back to Sicily, you could make a good profit from making up-time-style knives, if you learn how. But first, we must get the stiletto business started here."

Crossing himself, Alessandro said, "Do not wish ill luck on me by saying I might leave this place so quickly. And you have not explained why Master Förster would let so many leave. Is his business doing poorly?"

Skip waved his hand around. "Pah yourself. I don't know why you came here! Maybe there's a girl waiting who won't leave our warm home for cold Grantville, even with central heating. Grantville is *not* a cheap place to do business. It can be highly profitable, but never cheap. Even a half-day ride from here, doing business is cheaper. There are tons of reasons people leave Grantville after a year or two." He shrugged. "It's not wishing 'ill luck' on you, it's just how it is."

Alessandro grunted but dropped his hands to his lap and physically relaxed a bit more.

"Besides, Alessandro, Grantville is the most famous place now. Saying you have a business in Commerce or were trained there isn't going to impress people anywhere else like saying Grantville would. So, Master Förster—and virtually every other business—has more skilled applicants than they can employ. You hiring a few of his employees lets him hire new ones *and* know one of 'his guys' has a solid business that isn't competing with him. Win-win, as they say here. Since more new apprentices and journeymen will be able to say they are Grantville-trained, it's a win-win-win."

"Hmph." Alessandro's booted feet dropped to the wooden floor with a solid thud as he leaned forward and gulped down the last of his rapidly cooling tea. Heaving himself to his feet, Alessandro grabbed his bag and headed toward the bedroom doors, talking over his shoulder. "Where do I put my things?"

Skip jumped up. "Hold on there! This is only housing for high-school students. I have to move out in June, when I graduate. Let's go see Master Förster about where you should stay. I didn't expect you yet, but someone at his shop should know."

In no mood to dilly-dally, Alessandro turned on his heel and headed back toward the door. Stopping, he pulled another coat from its peg and tossed it to Skip. "Let's go meet this smith and see what I have gotten myself into."

Helmut's Forge, Grantville

The small apprentice shrank back into himself even further, as if afraid of being hit. In the noise of the forge, his voice seemed barely more than a whisper, although it was almost certainly strong enough to be heard easily in any other place. "I don't know where Master Förster is. He has much business to do."

Agostino Bellini wasn't an old Grantville hand, but he wasn't a fresh arrival either. Soon after credible news of the Grantville marvels reached Brindisi, Agostino's extended family decided one of the younger generation must go there to learn and secure their future. He was just young enough to not have an apprenticeship and well-behaved enough for his family to take a chance sending him. It never occurred to Agostino's family to ask his opinion. If they had, they might have realized he lacked the bold spirit such an adventure called for. Given the chance to go anywhere in the world, he would have chosen to stay in Brindisi. In his own house in Brindisi. Possibly in his own bed in his own house in Brindisi. Under no circumstances would he have gone somewhere loud, cold, and far, far away where they spoke not one but three foreign languages—English, German, and Amideutsch.

But they didn't ask him what he wanted. Instead, they sent him to live with a cousin in Venice where he worked running errands for up-timers who came through the city, allowing him to start learning up-timer English and Amideutsch. Once he was reasonably fluent, they sent him to Grantville with a merchant's caravan.

Seeing the two older boys, or perhaps men, weren't leaving, Agostino left out a sigh, shoulders drooping. "I will search for our senior journeyman, Zacharias. He is in charge when Master Förster is not here. He can help you."

Skip nodded his thanks and understanding as Agostino went into the forge proper, leaving them waiting in the much cooler area near the front office.

***

Ten minutes later, a solidly muscled young man walked through the door, wiping his face with a small towel he tucked into the rear waist of his leather apron. "I'd shake your hands, but," he wiggled his stained fingers, "mine aren't exactly pristine." Alessandro's brow knit at the last word. "Ah, English is still new to you. I mean they aren't as clean as they could be. I can't promise to help you, but I'll do my best. What's up?"

As Alessandro rocked back, brows knit tight, Skip suppressed a wince. *I forgot how bad Alessandro always was with other languages. He doesn't have an ear for it, at all.* "Thanks. Zacharias, is it?"

"Yes, but the up-timers have shortened it to Zach."

Seeing the fleeting sadness cross Zach's face, Skip couldn't help but laugh. "Please. Do not take offense. I truly understand your distress." He held out his hand. "My name was Scipione, now shortened to Skip. Yours is much better!"

The tension melted out of Zach as he smiled and gave a nod of understanding.

"Now, to our business. I have spoken to your master about having a Sicilian master stiletto maker work in this space. Alessandro is that master, but he arrived sooner than expected, and I need to figure out where he can stay. Since I didn't expect him yet, we hadn't finalized those arrangements."

"Ah, yes! I have heard of this. I am to work with him, as is young Tino, the apprentice who came to find me. He is from southern Italy, the far Eastern part of the boot heel, so the hope was that perhaps he and your Sicilian master could speak more easily with each other, since so few speak English or German there. He is still quite a young apprentice and has few skills, but he is a good lad." He turned to address Alessandro directly. "Tell me, please, how someone so young is a master of enough standing to come here."

Skip answered for him. "He isn't. A master of high standing, that is. Our town has no space for another master, nor do they know of a space for him nearby. Yet he has the skills to be a master. A young woman and both their families await his gaining enough stability for an official betrothal. When I found this business opportunity, possibly his *only* opportunity to have his own business and start his life soon, Alessandro came here as a brand-new *klingenmeister.*"

Zach's body was as still as a statue as his head rotated toward Skip, eyes narrowed. "And now perhaps you can tell me why *you* are answering the questions while this 'master' remains silent."

"Have you ever met a person who can pick up a language so quickly it astounds everyone? The kind of person who can mimic a language so perfectly that in mere months they sound like a native?"

Zach nodded.

"Does it not make sense that there would be people who are the opposite of that? Those who even after years of living in a place have an accent so thick it is difficult to understand them? Who never truly become comfortable in another language?"

"Ah. So, you are saying that he is unable to converse easily in any language except the one he was born to?" Skip nodded. "Then it is indeed a good thing we have young Tino here, assuming they can converse."

Skip took a moment to quickly translate the conversation up to this point for Alessandro, who had only understood fragments of it. Turning back to Zach, he motioned toward the other room. "Can the young man–Tino?–come back? You are right that Alessandro speaks little other than our local tongue. He has never had an ear for language. I didn't truly realize how poor before tonight. If Tino cannot help him, we will need to find another way."

As Tino walked back into the room, Skip started talking to him in Sicilian. He straightened up and chattered back in his native tongue, thrilled to finally be able to talk freely to someone. There were differences, but it was close enough for Tino and Alessandro to communicate easily.

Five minutes later, Skip moved to the side, allowing Alessandro and Tino to continue their conversation. "Zach, I really do need to figure out where he's staying and get him there. I have homework waiting for me and a test tomorrow that I haven't studied enough for. Do you have any idea what they had in mind? Or do I need to find a room for him somewhere?"

Zach pulled a clipboard out of the gray bag slung over his shoulder. "These papers were being prepared for him. You can read them, but it says that he will work for Summer's Kitchen at least twenty hours per week. In exchange, he can stay in the subsidized housing the company set up for employees and earn a little money. For him, the housing is the main benefit.

If he finds somewhere else to live and moves out, that's fine, but this seemed like a good way to get settled here."

He looked to the side. "Tino, can you explain this to Alessandro please?" Seeing the lad's nod, he continued talking to Skip. "It will also help him get to know some of the apprentices and other staff better. That's important too."

Keeping an eye on Alessandro, Skip nodded. "Makes sense. I think that will be good, so I'll talk to him for a minute then head back to my room to study. Can someone make sure he gets dinner and settles in? Thanks."

Zach headed across the cluttered room, putting his left arm around Alessandro's shoulders and guiding him toward the smithy, where he could observe the operation, put down his tools, and meet the workers. He waved goodbye with his right arm without turning around as he, Alessandro, and Tino walked through the door into the smithy.

Marcantonio's Pizza
March 1637

"Pizza *cu* pepperoni." Alessandro's mouth twisted as he realized he had used the Sicilian word for "with" instead of the English. Again. Alessandro pulled out his wallet as Skip paid. He snarled, "I am not a child. I can pay for my own meal."

One black eyebrow disappeared into Skip's neatly cut and styled hair. "Indeed. But this is a *business* meal, making it a *business* expense, so the *business* is paying for us both. And we shall be discussing business." Skip gave a single curt nod as Alessandro settled into the booth. "Also, we shall speak in Sicilian."

Alessandro tried to stand, getting slightly stuck in the still-unfamiliar booth, his face turning increasingly red from embarrassment and frustration. Skip finally shoved his chest just hard enough to push him back into the seat. "Calm down. It's not your language skills. How many people here do you think are fluent in Sicilian? There might be one or two, but they probably won't be close enough to hear us. Most could listen to our whole conversation if it was in a more common language. So, we stick to our native tongue."

Alessandro finally grunted his acknowledgement. "Fine. I don't understand how everyone else can learn all these accursed other tongues so easily. And so quickly!" The tabletop wobbled from his fist striking it.

"Calm down. Seriously. You are strong, and we do not want to pay to fix or replace an up-time table. As for people learning languages quickly, up-timers have studied lots of things. The younger you are when you try to learn a new language, the easier it is, and many who move here are young. I'm guessing most people who don't like learning other languages just don't come here. Tino and Zach both told me that your Amideutsch is improving, but your German... Your German is..."

"Lousy. Nearly non-existent. Not improving fast enough to even take a basic order. Amazingly, even worse than my English, which is pretty bad. So yeah, I'm doing better at Amideutsch than the other local languages. But I still have to keep an apprentice with me when I'm doing business." He took a long drink of beer. "Do you have any idea how humiliating that is?"

"Put a pin in that. I'll be right back." Skip went over to the counter and flirted with the young woman behind the counter before picking up the tray with their food, utensils, and pure white cloth napkins.

"What do you mean telling me to put a pin in it?"

"It means to hold onto an idea for later while the conversation moves onto something else. Like using a pin to hold a piece of paper in place until later."

"Am I such an idiot that you need to explain that to me? Why is my humiliation so unimportant it can't be discussed until later?"

Skip fixed him with a glare. "Because pizza is best eaten hot, no matter how many people are happy to eat it cold, and I wanted to be settled with our food before starting to discuss it. But since that's too much to ask of you, it does sound humiliating. Pass the red pepper flakes. Sucks for you to be that lousy at languages. You aren't the only one who needs a translator to do business in Grantville. I'm always impressed by how white the napkins are. My friends tell me that they bleach them regularly, which is why they stick with white. Same logic for the doctor's lab coats and surgical clothing at up-time-style hospitals. Some of my classmates work as translators for businessmen in Grantville. There is *always* work." He paused and looked down at his slice. "It definitely needs parmesan. Do you need anything from the counter?"

Alessandro shook his head no. When Skip slid back into his seat, Alessandro said, "Fine. You win. You weren't being a dick. We can 'put a pin in it' while we eat. Happy?"

Skip fairly beamed around a big mouthful of supreme as he saluted with a mug of fresh, room-temperature beer.

Ten minutes later, Skip stacked both plates with the utensils and napkins, then put them at the end of the table and moved the unfinished pizza slightly. "I'll take the rest with us when we leave. Now, to business. Yes, your language skills suck. That's not a shock. It's okay. Lots of people are new to Grantville, and hardly anyone is fluent in English when they arrive. The few who *are* fluent know 1630s English, not up-timer English. So, stop stressing."

"Do not treat me like a child. They learn. I'm not *learning*. I'm stuck."

"Don't *act* like a child. You aren't stuck. You just suck. Your progress is slow, but it's there. Focus on the Amideutsch. There aren't as many words.

Don't bother with German. Learn enough English to run the business. Focus on words for smithing. That's all you need for now."

Alessandro stared at a poster of up-time Italy behind the counter the entire time Skip spoke. As the silence grew, he pushed back from the table until his back was straight against the seat. A single terse nod.

"Now that we covered that, how is the smith doing? Are there any apprentices or journeymen you want to hire?"

Alessandro crossed his arms. "Tino is good enough to keep. So is Zach. Jorg. Erhert. Maybe Mertin or Lorentz. I've narrowed it down, but I still have three months."

"The knives you brought sold really well, but now the women are asking about some kind of scabbard." As the door tinkled, Skip looked at his watch, then the door. "And there is the second half of our meeting." He rose and waved the man over, switching to English as he motioned to the remains of the pizza. "Gebhard! Thank you for meeting us, please have a slice while we talk. I just told Alessandro women have been asking about scabbards, which is where you come in."

Speaking around a mouthful of pizza, Gebhard pulled out a sketchpad. "These are my ideas. First, a thigh holster for a stiletto with straps around the thigh at the top and bottom. Another strap at the top goes to a waistband. No elastic or other up-time materials needed, and it stays in place." He turned the page. "I have lots of other ideas, but it really comes back to this. It's practical, easy to make, and inexpensive. Most importantly, it works with most outfits. Sure, a few up-time dresses are too tight and something like this would print and be too hard to reach, but there aren't many like that."

He stood up and removed his coat, hanging it at the end of the booth. He motioned to a young woman who had walked in with him. She took off her jacket, then twirled, so they could see there weren't any visible weapons. As she stopped, she slipped her hand into a pocket, pulled out a stiletto, laid it on the table next to Gebhard's plate, grabbed her coat, and walked out the front door. The whole thing happened so fast that most of the other patrons didn't notice.

Looking after her consideringly, Alessandro turned his attention back to the sketch. "*Is gut.*"

"Thanks. I'm pretty happy with it. I've sold a dozen so far." Gebhard reached out and made the small knife disappear.

"Fantastic! Alessandro has the first new knives finished by one of the journeymen and several more he's made. I'd love to package them with your conceal-carry garters. What do you think?"

Gebhard pulled a box out of his coat pocket. Wiping a small, residual smear of grease from the tabletop with a napkin, he placed the box in the center of the table before removing the lid with a flourish. "It is a superior idea!" Inside the flat silver box, on top of red satin, the stiletto knife from the table now nestled next to a garter. Alessandro reverently reached out to touch the box. A smile played about his lips as he looked up at Gebhard before bursting into deep belly laughs.

Speaking Sicilian, he told Skip, "Tell the man. It is nearly perfect. But the box should be the color of skin since the inside is blood red." Gebhard's broad smile indicated his agreement. Despite the language barrier, they had reached an agreement.

July 1637

Dejected, Alessandro huddled on a bench in the middle of Hough Park with Tino. "It is a sunny summer afternoon, but it feels more like a winter afternoon." He shuddered as if a chill had swept over him. This was not the first time the two of them had commiserated, complained, and kvetched about how much colder northern Europe during the Little Ice Age was than their native Southern Italy.

Letting his hands (and lunch) drop to his lap, Tino looked every bit as miserable as Alessandro. "Winter here is truly an awful thing but my family has said I must 'stay to find the opportunity for my future.'"

"My family has also said I must stay to ensure my future. I promised to stay for a year to get this business going but the cold makes it very hard to stay." As he ate the kimchee from his lunch, his tension melted away and he nearly smiled. "I have sent several recipes for this to my mother and my intended bride. I tried the sauerkraut. It also uses the extra cabbage, but is not as good as the kimchee." He looked at Tino's simple pasta salad. "You should try more of the foods they have. Many are quite good."

Tino giggled. "I tried their 'Italian' food once. It was so bad! Nothing like Mama makes."

Seeing Skip leave the public pool and head toward them, Alessandro stood and held out a hand toward Tino. "Okay. Not the Italian food, then, but have you had a bagel? I will take you to the Golden Pagoda before I leave. Chinese food is like nothing else you have ever eaten."

Refusing to ever live up to his nickname, Skip made sure to run (*not* skip) toward his business partner. "It's July! Why are you wearing a sweater?"

"It's cold. Why are you swimming in almost no clothing?"

Skip clapped Alessandro on the back, propelling him exactly nowhere. Weak, easily maneuvered men did poorly in a smithy. But Alessandro took the hint and moved toward the bridge over the Buffalo Creek and back toward downtown. Reaching into the unbleached linen and wool backpack Tino was carrying, Alessandro handed Skip a small financial ledger.

As they approached the High Street bridge, Skip handed the ledger back. "There's a bench up ahead. We'll sit there while we talk. I wish I could say this looked great, but it doesn't. We're barely making a fifty percent profit after costs."

Skip stumbled as Alessandro stopped in front of him. "Barely fifty percent? Not great? You really are a child, aren't you?"

Resuming his original pace, Skip didn't say a word as he walked to the bench and sat, lips compressed so hard they were a slash across his face. His words and tone tight, he spoke. "I am not a child. I have lived in Grantville long enough to understand how much a truly successful business makes, and it is a great deal more than fifty percent. *In Grantville*, this is a failure. At home it might be a success, but we aren't *at* home, are we?"

Stunned, Alessandro hit back. "This town is crazy! How is this possibly a failure? I cannot do this. I cannot live in a place where the warmest days feel like winter and a successful business is branded a failure. This is too much. The only thing keeping me here is the business being a success, and now you tell me it is a failure!"

Skip looked at him, nonplused. "Don't overreact. It's fine."

Alessandro snapped, "It is not *fine*. It is a *failure*, in your own words. Or perhaps *I* am the failure, not the business, and I should sell and leave." He stood and stalked back toward his living quarters, leaving Alessandro staring open-mouthed at his retreating back.

Two Weeks Later
Slate Lane Stables

Looking contrite, Skip tried one last time. "Isn't there something I can say to change your mind?"

"Even if there was, I sold Zach my share of the business. Tino's family sent permission for him to come with me, since I agree he is my apprentice and will become my journeyman. Lorentz is coming as well, at his own expense. He hates winter nearly as much as I do and wants to try real Italian food. I have enough money to start my own smithy. I can make genuine up-time kitchen knives, and I have a journeyman and an apprentice trained in making those as well.

"I want to get married. I have not been in Grantville for a full year, but by the time I can get home, I will have been gone for a year. More importantly, I have earned enough to start my own shop, once I sell the business here. Less than if I stayed until spring, but I'm done. I studied up-time knives and learned how to make what the up-timers called a 'switchblade.' No one else within hundreds of miles of Sicily will know this, and I can make the up-time kitchen knives, so my new shop should do well.

"But most of all, Grantville is cold and learning new languages is hard. I do not want to be trapped here for another winter. I want to go home where I can understand what everyone is saying, and people don't hang out near the forge to get warm." Alessandro grabbed Skip in a giant bear hug, picking him up off the floor. "Goodbye, my young friend. I will never forget what you have done for me."

Author's Note:

If you are interested in learning more about the history of the stiletto (blade), this is a fascinating article on the topic. (If you can't open the link, Wikipedia seems to have simply copied the text at https://en.wikipedia.org/wiki/Stiletto.)

https://jairusnadabusa.medium.com/the-history-and-evolution-of-italian-stiletto-thrusting-knife-ea18fe51264b

https://tsprof.us/blogs/news/italian-stiletto-history-and-modernity

For a brief history of the stiletto (shoe), read this. The key point: they couldn't be made until steel was available for the heels. Materials technology had to advance well past where it was in the seventeenth century to create them.

https://www.popsci.com/science-stiletto-heel-shoes/

News and New Books
Available Now, Coming Soon, and FenCon

Flint's Shards, Inc.

Available Now

1635: The Weavers Code, The Private Casefiles of Archie Gottesfreund, Legions of Pestilence, The Trouble with Huguenots, Things Could be Worse, Designed to Fail, The Unexpected Sales Rep

1635: The Weaver's Code
Eric Flint and Jody Lynn Nye

A young gentlewoman, Margaret de Beauchamp, finds her fate twisted into the lives of the up-timers when she meets the Americans imprisoned in the Tower of London. In exchange for her help, Rita Simpson and Harry Lefferts give her a huge sum of money to keep her family's manor and its woolen trade from falling into the hands of the crown and its unscrupulous minister, Lord Cork. But Margaret's troubles are not at an end. Her family's fortunes are in a downward spiral. Her trip to Grantville brings unexpected dangers and a possible up-time solution.

Inspired by books in the Grantville library, Margaret has an idea to restore her family's fortunes with an innovation never before seen in fabric design. With the help of Aaron Craig, an up-timer programmer using aqualators, water-powered computers, they teach her father's craftsmen to create a combination machine loom that can produce a new type of woolen cloth. The ornate and perfect patterns quickly trend among the nobility. However, the Master Weavers of the county's Weaver's Guild aren't happy about being overshadowed by the changes to the status quo, and take their grievance to Lord Cork, who is still looking for the people who helped the Americans escape from the Tower.

Cork isn't interested in squabbles between mere tradesmen, but he is very interested in taking over the new calculating machine that is fueling the upsurge in the de Beauchamp fortunes. He sends agents ordered to stop at nothing to secure it for his own ends. Margaret has to protect her new business, and prevent anyone from discovering that up-timers are in the country to assist her, but she still has to deal with an uprising at home.

https://www.baen.com/1635-the-weaver-s-code.html

The Private Casefiles of Archie Gottesfreund
David Carrico

New detective and adventure stories laid in the Ring of Fire Universe.

Archibald Gottesfreund, a half-Scot/half-German mercenary, retired from that life after losing both his cousin Rory and part of his own left hand in a skirmish with brigands in northern France. Weary of that life, Archie rode east, looking for a new life, which he found in Jena when he met up with Master Tiberius Claudius Titus Wulff. After doing the master merchant a favor, he found himself enlisted to be Master Titus' chief agent and right-hand man, a life he never expected.

Over the years, Master Titus' business affairs and his passion for books alike provide many adventures for Archie. Two of the best are presented in this volume.

Legions of Pestilence
Virginia DeMarce

"In the world the West Virginians of Grantville came from, the borderlands between France and Germany had been a source of turmoil for centuries. In the new universe created by the Ring of Fire, the situation isn't any better. The chaotic condition of the German lands has been ended--for a time, at least. And the near-century long war between Spain and the Netherlands has finally been resolved.

But now France is unstable. The defeat of Richelieu's forces in the Ostend War has weakened the Red Cardinal's grip on political power and emboldened his enemies. Foremost among them is King Louis XIII's ambitious younger brother, Monsieur Gaston. An inveterate schemer and would-be usurper, Gaston's response to the new conditions in France is to launch a military adventure. He invades the Duchy of Lorraine. Soon, others are drawn into the conflict. The Low Countries ruled by King Ferdinand and Duke Bernhard's newly formed Burgundy, a king-dom-in-all-but-name, send their own troops into Lorraine. Chaos expands and spreads up and down the Rhine.

It isn't long before the mightiest and most deadly army enters the fray--the legions of pestilence. Bubonic plague and typhus lead the way, but others soon follow: dysentery, deadly and disfiguring smallpox, along with new diseases introduced by the time-displaced town of Grantville. The war is on. All the wars--and on all fronts. Can the medical knowledge of the up-time Americans be adapted and spread fast enough to forestall disaster? Or will their advanced military technology simply win one war in order to lose the other and much more terrible one?"

https://www.baen.com/legions-of-pestilence.html

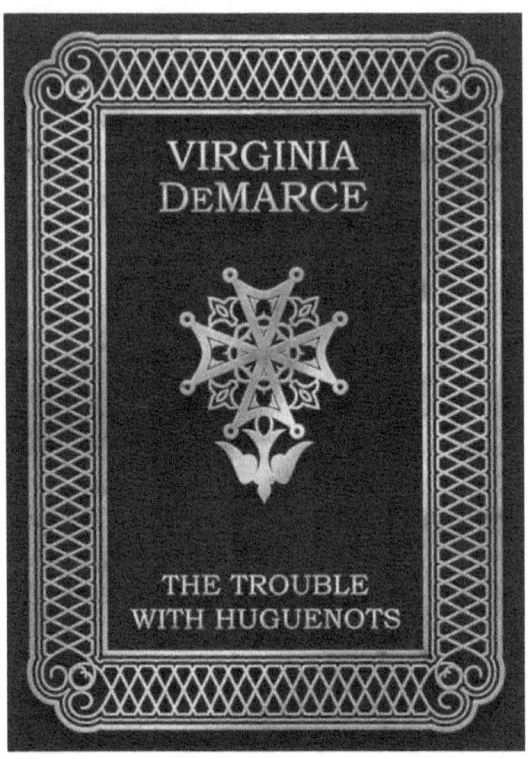

The Trouble with Huguenots
Virginia DeMarce

Ever since the assassination of King Louis XIII and the overthrow of his chief minister, Cardinal Richelieu, France has been in political and military turmoil. The possibility—even the likelihood—of revolution hovers in the background. The new king, Gaston, whom many consider a usurper, is no friend of France's Protestants, known as the Huguenots. The fears and hostility of the Huguenots toward the French crown have only been heightened by the knowledge brought back in time by the Americans of the town of Grantville. Half a century in the future, the French king of the time would revoke the Edict of Nantes of 1598, which proclaimed that the rights of Huguenots would be respected. At the center of all this turmoil is the universally recognized leader of the Huguenots: Duke Henri de Rohan. He knows from the same up-time history books that he is "scheduled" to die less than two years in the future and he has pressing problem on his hands. His estranged wife and brother are siding with the usurper Gaston and plotting against him. Still worse, his sole child and heir is his nineteen-year-old daughter Marguerite. He believes he has less than two years to find a suitable husband for her—but acceptable Calvinist noblemen, French or foreign, are sparse at the moment. What's a father to do?

https://www.baen.com/the-trouble-with-huguenots-demarce.html

Things Could Be Worse
Virginia DeMarce

The Ring of Fire that transported the town of Grantville from West Virginia in the year 2000 to the region of Thuringia in the middle of Europe in the year 1631 produced an enormous cascade of changes in world history. Some of those changes were big, others were huge—and some were more modest in scale. Modest, at the least, to the universe, if not necessarily to those immediately affected.

Count Ludwig Guenther of Schwarzburg-Rudolstadt builds a Lutheran church on his own land, not far from Grantville, and calls in a Saxon pastor of a Philippist bent to serve the Lutheran refugee population of the area. Shortly thereafter, in April 1634, the pastor's older daughter meets and elopes with a Catholic up-timer, which prompts Kastenmayer to get Lutheran girls to marry unchurched up-timers and thereby recruit them into the parish.

In the years that follow, Pastor Kastenmayer copes with both existing ecclesio-political strands of down-time religion (from Stiefelite Lutheran heretics to Flacian Lutheran ultra-orthodox) and the strange new up-time world of shorts, blue jeans, and unknown religious denominations. His struggles and travails have a surprisingly revolutionary impact on seventeenth-century Lutheranism—perhaps to no one's greater surprise than the pastor himself.

https://www.baen.com/things-could-be-worse-demarce.html

The Unexpected Sales Reps
Virginia DeMarce

How to succeed at spying without really trying.

Pranksters and scammers from way back, Paolo Fucilla and Carlo Rigatti fought for Spain at the Wartburg and survived.

Curious about the people who had beaten them so handily, they went to Grantville. Whatever their other faults, they were serious about keeping their oaths. When they promised not to take up arms they meant it. In Grantville, they got in trouble again and skipped town.

Looking for a job that didn't include being shot at with napalm, they decided to try their hand at spying. It was a "Here, hold my beer and watch this" inspiration. It wasn't their first, and it wouldn't be their last.

They went to work for the Archbishop of Salzburg. But spies need cover stories, so they decided to sell office supplies. It was supposed to be a single job, so they didn't bother to tell the manufacturer that they were now the sales reps for Vignelli Business Machines.

Watch as Paolo and Carlo demonstrate the kind of trouble they can get into.

https://www.baen.com/september-ebook-tbd.html

Designed To Fail
Virginia DeMarce

Frederik of Denmark, the son of King Christian IV, is the new governor of the new province of Westphalia and harbors the dark suspicion that the Swedes who now dominate central Europe deliberately designed the province so that he would not succeed in his assignment, thus undermining his father's position. Problems are everywhere! Religious fragmentation, cities demanding imperial status, jurisdictional disputes among the nobility and between the nobility and the common folk—there's no end to it.

And then matters get still more complicated. Annalise Richter, a student at the famous Abbey of Quedlinburg, wants Frederik to correct an injustice. Her mentor, the Abbess of Quedlinburg, is being prevented from running for a seat in the House of Commons because she is, well, not a commoner. Surely Frederik can do something to fix this wrong! The prince is of two minds. On the one hand—being very much his father's son—he has developed a great passion for the marvelous young woman. He is determined to marry her. On the other hand . . . she's Catholic. A bit of a problem, that, for a Lutheran prince. But there's worse. She's also the younger sister of Gretchen Richter. Yes, that Gretchen Richter.

https://www.baen.com/designed-to-fail.html

Coming Soon

1637: The French Correction, 1637: The
Pacific Initiative

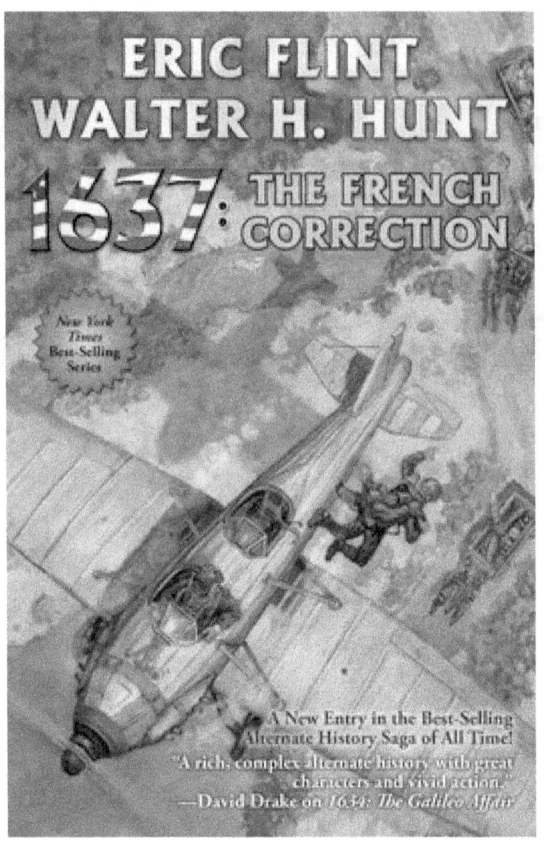

1637: The French Correction
Eric Flint & Walter Hunt

NEW RING OF FIRE SERIES ENTRY FROM THE LATE ERIC FLINT AND BEST-SELLING AUTHOR WALTER HUNT: The King is dead: Long Live the King. But which one? Gaston sits on the throne in Paris, but the dead king's infant son has powerful forces on his side, ready to place him where he belongs. Who will prevail?

Tensions build in France following the ascension of Gaston to the throne of his murdered brother, but there are factions supporting the claim of King Louis' surviving infant son. As France moves toward civil war, other parties, both visible and invisible, maneuver to take advantage of the increased tension. Who will survive to reign over France—King Gaston, the exiled child and his regents, or the King of Spain?

Coming March 4, 2025

1637: The Pacific Initiative
Iver P. Cooper

NEW RING OF FIRE SERIES ENTRY FROM IVER P. COOPER: A cosmic catastrophe, the Ring of Fire, strands the West Virginia town of Grantville back in time in the middle of the Thirty Years War. One of its ripple effects is that Japan has pulled back from a policy of isolation and staked out its own claims on the west coast of North America. But it is not the only power interested in that part of the New World, and the native Americans have also responded, in different ways, to the unexpected colonists. And there are conflicts among the colonists themselves.

In settling the fate of this part of the New World, a few remarkable individuals have an outsize role to play: Oyamada Isamu, a samurai on his first independent command; Yells-at-Bears, a young native woman of Vancouver Island; Father Blanco, a Jesuit priest and former missionary; and Iroha Data-hime, the daughter of the Grand Governor of New Nippon.

Coming March 4, 2025

1632 at FenCon

In 2025, 1632Con will be at Fencon in Dallas, Texas, February 14-16.

It's the twenty-fifth anniversary of 1632, and Fencon's twentieth.

Register for the con and hotel here:

http://www.fencon.org/

Don't forget your travel arrangements!

Toni Weisskopf is the toastmaster, and Kevin Ikenberry (Assiti Shards novel *The Crossing*) is the special workshop guest.

1632Con travels from con to con to give everyone a chance to attend.

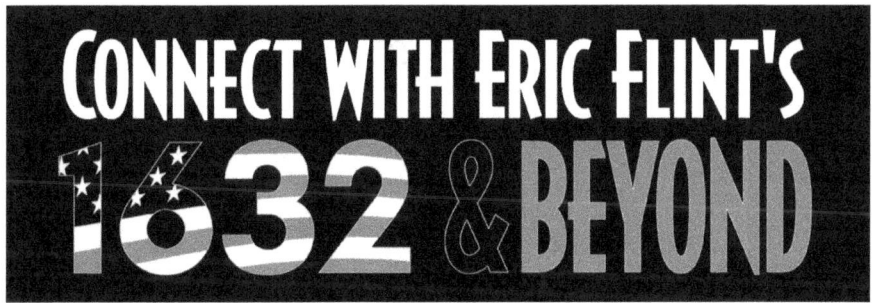

Connect with Eric Flint's 1632 & Beyond

W e would love to hear from you here at *Eric Flint's 1632 & Beyond!* There are lots of ways to get in touch with us and we look forward to hearing from you.

Main Sites

Email: 1632Magazine@1632Magazine.com

Shop: 1632Magazine.com

Author Site: Author.1632Magazine.com

For anyone interested in writing in the 1632verse, or fans interested in more background on the series and how we keep track of everything.

***

Social Media

Our Facebook Group is our primary social media, but we do use the FB Page, YouTube, and Instagram accounts.

Facebook Group: The Grantville Gazette / 1632 & Beyond

YouTube: 1632andBeyond

Facebook Page: Facebook.com/t1632andBeyond

***

Reviews and More

Because reviews really do matter, especially for small publishers and indie authors, please take a few minutes to post a review on Amazon, Goodreads, or wherever you find books, and don't forget to tell your friends to check us out!

You are welcome to join us on **BaensBar.net**. Most of the chatting about 1632 on the Bar is in the 1632 Tech forum. If you want to read and comment on possible future stories, check out 1632 Slush (stories) and 1632 Slush Comments on BaensBar.net.

If you are interested in writing in the 1632 universe, that's fabulous! Please visit **Author.1632Magazine.com** (QR code above) for more information.

www.ingramcontent.com/pod-product-compliance
Lightning Source LLC
Chambersburg PA
CBHW051437170626
46809CB00006B/2497